DEAD LOSS

*Joan Lock titles available from
Severn House Large Print*

Dead End
Dead Fall
Dead Letters

DEAD LOSS

Joan Lock

Severn House Large Print
London & New York

This first large print edition published in Great Britain 2006 by
SEVERN HOUSE LARGE PRINT BOOKS LTD of
9-15 High Street, Sutton, Surrey, SM1 1DF.
First world regular print edition published 2006 by
Severn House Publishers, London and New York.
This first large print edition published in the USA 2006 by
SEVERN HOUSE PUBLISHERS INC., of
595 Madison Avenue, New York, NY 10022.

British Library Cataloguing in Publication Data

Lock, Joan
  Dead loss. - Large print ed. - (A Detective Inspector Best
  Victorian mystery)
  1. Best, Ernest (Fictitious character) - Fiction 2. Police
  - England - London - Fiction 3. Bombings - England - London
  - History - 19th century - Fiction 4. London (England) -
  Social conditions - 19th century - Fiction 5. Detective and
  mystery stories 6. Large type books
  I. Title
  823.9'14[F]

ISBN-13: 9780727875594
ISBN-10: 0727875590

Printed and bound in Great Britain by
MPG Books Ltd, Bodmin, Cornwall.

To David and Gloria Luck

One

The letter was heart-rending. Even to readers whose hearts it was not intended to touch. Perhaps particularly so for those readers, reaching out as it did from the staid personal columns of the *Daily News*:

Dear F,
I implore you to give me help in this hour of my deepest trial. Friendless and ill, I can look to none but you. I am helpless without you. By the memory of the happy past I entreat your aid, or I know not what I shall do.
My last shilling will pay for this advertisement. O remember me at this season of reunion. I have no home now, so please address to G.C., care of 14 Mitre Court, Fleet Street.

It was midwinter. The worst time of year to be in need. The season of reunion was, of course, Christmas, which was almost upon us.

7

Who could F be, wondered Detective Inspector Ernest Best. A married lover? A wayward son? A husband who had deserted her? That the writer was a woman he had no doubt: 'entreat' and 'implore' were scarcely words a man would use. They were more the pleas of a weak woman. And what man would confess 'I am helpless without you'?

He was quite aware that a woman was more likely to find herself in such a desperate situation. It was harder for them to find work, particularly if they were educated and had never worked before, which he sensed could be the case with this writer. 'The hour of my deepest trial' and 'this season of reunion' were hardly expressions used by scullery maids.

It just so happened that when he read this pathetic letter Best was actually *in* Fleet Street, partaking of a pint of beer at the Printers' Arms public house. It was all in the cause of duty; he was shadowing a suspect. But after his task was taken over by another officer and he was walking away along Fleet Street he decided to take the turning which led down into Mitre Court.

As he expected, number fourteen was an accommodation address, and one which was obviously experiencing a lull in business. This meant that the pale, bored-looking young man at the desk was more than happy to engage in light conversation.

He soon revealed that the letters addressed to G.C. were collected by a pretty young lady. 'There 'asn't 'alf been a lot of them,' he exclaimed, then added sadly, 'She seems to be in a lot of trouble.'

That news gave Best pause. Was he mistaken then in his suspicion that this was merely another newspaper-advertisement fraud? He knew that detectives who witnessed every kind of iniquity over a number of years' service could become cynical and suspicious. When not guarded against these could become ugly, dominant traits, as his wife, Helen, was fond of pointing out.

Helen was right, he decided. He must try to be more charitable. Give people the benefit of the doubt. The young lady seemed to be in a lot of trouble and it was the season of goodwill, all the more reason why he should be magnanimous.

His Christmas promised to be the best ever. He was, at last, happy, with his new wife Helen and the light-of-his-life, two-year-old Lucy Jane. What a stark contrast to the lot of this poor young woman, G.C.

'She ain't been in for two days,' the pale young man said, turning to point to a substantial stack of letters piled up in the slot of a rack on the wall behind him. 'I 'ope she's all right.'

Young men, indeed any men, were susceptible to a pretty face, but Best caught his concern and he too began to hope that G.C. had not come to any harm, had not given up hope when the one letter she wanted had not arrived. The River Thames was close by. At this time of year more desperate souls than ever gave up hope of finding room at the inn and instead made their way down to that unforgiving river.

Good heavens, I'm getting maudlin, thought Best. He reminded himself that it was just a little curious that there had been so many replies to a letter from a woman who claimed to be so alone.

He pulled himself up and made his way to the offices of the *Daily News*, which, as this was Fleet Street, the home of almost every newspaper and magazine in the land, was close by. He presented himself and his warrant card at the counter where the advertisements were placed and asked to see the original copy.

The sight of the handwritten note gave him a jolt. Then he began to grin. The hand which had penned the sad words in large black letters on expensive cream-laid writing paper was not the least bit girlish. Neither did it have the firmness of a more mature female – some motherly creature who might have kindly placed it on G.C.'s behalf.

No, it was clear to Best, who was something of an authority on the subject, that the letter had quite definitely been written by a man.

Two

Best was eager to follow up the matter of poor G.C., but knew he had little hope of doing so. A couple of years earlier he might have. But not now.

Not in these terrible times, when London was being held to ransom and its citizens were under constant threat of dreadful injury or even death. Scotland Yard detectives, indeed any police detectives, were needed to help prevent even more disasters and to guard the Queen and her ministers.

The terror had begun quite quietly back in January 1881, when, one densely foggy evening, an infernal machine was placed inside a ventilating grid in the wall of Salford army barracks. It duly exploded, injuring three passers-by, one of them seriously, and killing a seven-year-old child. That was the start of what was now known as the Dynamite War. Only it hadn't even *been* dynamite then, merely the much less deadly gunpowder.

The Home Secretary, who had been receiving alarming intelligence from the United States on plans to wage war in other British cities, most particularly London, communicated urgently with the CID Director, Howard Vincent. He was concerned, he declared, about the lack of local information on the whereabouts and movements of the Fenian organization in London.

'All other objects should be postponed in our efforts to get some light into these dark places,' he had insisted somewhat poetically. And postponed they were as the panic grew.

Kevin O'Brien, the man Best was shadowing in Fleet Street on this wintry December day, was thought to be a member of this organization, which was planning to bring more disaster upon London. However, he did not have the appearance of a person of any great purpose. Quite the opposite. He was a large, shambling sort of man wearing ill-fitting clothes, and was vague in both countenance and expression.

The vagueness of his countenance was due to a combination of totally unremarkable features, which blended into each other, and his almost colourless hair and eyes. Nature could scarcely have done a better job design-

12

ing a creature suitable for clandestine operations.

His habitual expression also was remarkable for its absence. Not a flicker of animation crossed his bland face as he sat eating his 'ordinary' – the regular set meal of the house – in a corner of the Printers' Arms. Best could not imagine this man planning his own day, let alone organizing an explosion by means of a fiendish device. But one thing Best had learned during his fifteen years' service was that you could never tell – about anything.

O'Brien was in the print, which meant, among other things, that his hours were irregular but his meal break wasn't, and this was why Best endeavoured to be at the Printers' Arms each morning at half-past eleven.

There he sat in the public bar nursing his pint, his head buried in yet another newspaper while O'Brien, an apparently solitary man, ate his meal. It was hoped that he might arrange a meeting with some suspicious character who, in turn, would lead them on to even more suspicious characters. But he never did.

Best dared not order food himself in case his quarry suddenly lost his appetite and left, although so far he had shown no signs of doing so. Indeed, he had shown no signs of doing anything.

He and Best had even developed the nodding acquaintance typical of regular clients in such establishments. It was not ideal that the man knew his face but to have not responded would have seemed strange. This nodding relationship did, however, mean that once outside, Best's usefulness as a shadower was compromised. A situation he did not regret. Shadowing was such a tedious yet tense business and one, in less fraught times, usually left to the lower ranks.

Thus he was quite happy that, when O'Brien left, a young City detective would take up the baton. It had been decided not to withdraw Best now that O'Brien knew him but, for the moment, to leave him to continue his pub vigil in case he was able to strike up a friendship with the man – accidentally. On no account should Best be seen to make the first move.

Best, irritated by this stalemate, was already compiling a mental list of possible 'accidents' and selecting the most suitable for his purpose.

Meanwhile, he began to notice that G.C. had somehow managed to scrape up another 'last shilling', indeed surely more than one, to ensure that her heartrending plea be given space in a variety of other leading newspapers.

Consequently, the next time he was relieved of his duty by the departure of O'Brien he once again decided to drop into G.C.'s accommodation address in nearby Mitre Court.

On this occasion, the pale young man was busy but he obviously recognized the foreign-looking Best, gave him a wave and, once his customers had gone, came over.

'It's all right!' he exclaimed. 'She's back!' Her arrival had obviously been something of an event in the young man's day.

'I'm relieved to hear it,' said Best. 'I've been worried about her.'

He nodded his mutual understanding.

'She comes in regular now. Every morning at 'alf past ten.'

He picked up a pile of letters and began sorting through them.

Best nodded at the pile. 'I hope there are still plenty for her to collect?'

'Oh, yes. More than ever!' He grinned. Then his thin fingers suddenly stopped sorting and he looked up. 'Mary isn't in any kind of trouble, is she?'

Oh. Mary, was it?

'No. Oh, no. I was just concerned about her.' Best spread his hands dramatically and assumed a pious expression. 'The weather this time of year can be so hard ... and after reading her distressing letter in the newspaper...'

The young man frowned, puzzled. 'The newspaper?' But before he could enquire further he was called away to another customer.

Best was tempted to ask for sight of Mary's letters but decided to hold back for now. After all, he had neither the proof that an offence had taken place nor the time to follow it up if it had.

He acknowledged that he was, in truth, merely indulging his curiosity so as to relieve the boredom of shadowing. It was a habit that had led him into many strange places and some alarming situations.

Three

Best could understand why the pale young man was so taken with Mary. She was one of those creamy, almost edible young women. Her body was soft and round, her cheeks peach-like and her liquid, dark brown eyes conveyed an air of childlike, fluttering helplessness melded with a hint of sexual promise. A delicious combination which could set men's pulses racing.

The morning conference at the Yard had finished early with a decision being made that this would be Best's last day at the Printers' Arms unless he and 'the mark' became friends. In which case it would be 'stet' – as you were – as they said in printing circles. But the move must come from O'Brien, not Best, he was told, and he could see little hope of that happening.

Set adrift from the office early he decided to get to Mitre Court by ten thirty and so make the acquaintance of Mary – from a distance.

When Best arrived she was already there. The pale young man nodded at him, glanced at the girl and seemed to be about to introduce them when Best shook his head and put his finger to his lips.

When she left, on an intoxicating wave of gardenia perfume, Best did also. An attractive quarry would make a nice change from a Fenian and there was hope of a more interesting outcome in this case.

The pursuit proved far from easy. The pavements of Fleet Street were narrow and bustled with life. Messengers, clerks, reporters and men from the print spilled out of newspaper offices to be joined by lawyers, with gowns flapping, as they emerged from the courts and alleyways leading from the ancient Inns of Court, their minions trailing them weighed down with boxes of papers and ribbon-tied legal briefs.

Best was almost knocked off his feet by an over-anxious messenger and then he became stuck behind two lawyers deep in a heated discussion. He heard torts, compensation and damages bandied around as he dodged back and forth trying to overtake them. When, finally, he emerged, Mary had gone.

He glanced around frantically and eventually glimpsed her tiny figure, encased in dark brown velvet, teetering uncertainly in the middle of the road. To get there she had dodged between carriages and carts and was now hesitating before attempting to complete the crossing.

Suddenly, she was off again, vainly trying to lift her skirts out of the mire. She was heading towards the newly completed Royal Courts of Justice, a gigantic, icing-sugar Gothic fantasy of a building where attempts were made to uphold civil law. Surely this could not be her destination?

It was not. She continued past the gaggle of newspaper reporters awaiting news of the outcome of latest financial or sexual scandal. She was walking quite fast but Best was now close behind her as she passed St Clement Danes Church, sitting incongruously on its tranquil island in the midst of the raging torrent of traffic.

She continued along into Wyche Street, passing the pit and gallery entrances of a pair of theatres known as 'the rickety twins'. The Opéra Comique and the Globe Theatre had been thrown up carelessly amidst the street's little old shops and houses by a building speculator hoping to gain compensation from the planned widening of the Strand and the fashioning of the Aldwych. Unfortunately for him, the project had been much postponed and the twins were now in grave danger of falling down, hence their nickname.

Mary scarcely slowed as she crossed Newcastle Street and carried on into the southern end of Drury Lane. Best took out his watch. It was twenty minutes past eleven. He hesitated, torn. He was supposed to be back at Fleet Street by eleven thirty but was loath to break off his pursuit at this stage. How much further was she going to go? If he left now he could get back in ten minutes, walking fast, but he would have to start soon.

She stopped suddenly to study the Olympic Theatre billboards advertising *She Stoops to Conquer* – rather appropriate given that the Olympic had the reputation of being a woman's theatre due to the number of ladies who had managed it since the great Madame Vestris began her reign in the 1830s.

Was Mary an actress? How appropriate if she were. She was already a dramatic damsel in distress in print and in real life to the pale young man. Though why she should waste her acting skills on him was a mystery. Perhaps it was in her nature? She couldn't help it? Some women couldn't, Best was given to understand. Or perhaps she did it in case another reader visited Mitre Court in the hope of seeing her there?

Why was she taking so long! It was no good, he would have to go back now. Suddenly she started off again then turned immediately right into Craven Buildings, which ran behind the theatre. She stopped before number 7, took out a key, opened the door and went in.

Best looked around to make sure no one was watching, approached the door and examined the nameplate alongside. He located the name of the landlord, Harrry Rice, turned around and headed back to Fleet Street almost at a run.

He had underestimated the time it would take and it was almost eleven forty-five by the time he finally puffed into the Printers' Arms. As he entered he automatically glanced over to the corner where O'Brien usually sat.

It was empty!

Oh my God! The man could be planting a bomb somewhere! People might die because he had wanted to indulge his curiosity about G.C.!

This year had been the worst so far for fiendish devices. It began in January in Glasgow with the attack on a gasometer, an explosion at a railway station coaling shed and a foiled attempt to breach the aqueduct which took the Forth and Clyde Canal over the city. In March had come attempts on *The Times'* newspaper offices and the Mansion House followed by the successful attack on government buildings close to Downing Street and the Houses of Parliament. Finally, in October, two bombs had exploded on the London underground railway. One, outside a carriage near Charing Cross Station, caused only limited damage but the other, at Praed Street Station, shattered three third-class carriages and a large gas main and injured some seventy-two people.

The 'war' was hotting up and the expertise of the bombers growing daily – and Best had let one of them out of his sight! He was still staring at the empty corner and cursing himself when the landlord asked, 'What are you having, then, sir?'

'I ... I...'

Should he dash out to try to find O'Brien? But where?

'Let me get one for you,' said a soft Irish voice behind him.

O'Brien!

'Er...'

'Your usual?' asked the landlord helpfully.

Best nodded dumbly. 'Yes, thanks. Thanks,' he managed eventually, making a brave attempt to appear casual.

'Kevin O'Brien,' said the Irishman holding out his hand. 'Time we became properly acquainted.'

'Ernest,' said Best. 'Ernest Halliday.'

'Thought I'd never get away today,' smiled O'Brien. 'Hell of a morning.'

Now that it was animated the man's face looked quite different. But why was he doing this? Did he know who Best was? Or was he guessing? 'I was surprised that you were not in your usual corner,' he laughed, deciding it would be sensible not to hide his interest. 'You're such a fixture there.'

'So I am,' said O'Brien. 'So I am. As regular as the early morning dew over the paddocks.' He looked Best in the eye. 'And so are you. Do you work around here?'

Four

'You been rumbled,' said Chief Inspector Cheadle in his blunt way.

Best shook his head. 'I don't know. I think he believed me when I said I was a writer for the *Wine Trade Gazette*.' He paused. He was hoping this might mean he would be taken off the shadowing duty. It was an ignominious way to finish his surveillance but a relief nonetheless.

'You should dress more...' Cheadle waved his large right hand about, searching for the word, 'more...'

'Soberly?' asked Best.

Cheadle grunted, pulling at the edges of his greying side whiskers. The old man had been dragged back from retirement because they were desperate for experienced officers to help handle this crisis.

'Well, in this case I think Ernest's appearance might be a good, *natural* disguise,' said Chief Superintendent Williamson, who did not approve of his men getting themselves up as cab drivers or butchers. He grinned.

'People expect us to be wearing size ten police boots and cheap, tight suits.'

'Mebbe,' grunted Cheadle. He didn't like to contradict his beloved chief. 'But when you dress flash you gets known for it. Then you're done for.'

'When you are dealing with *criminals*, perhaps,' Williamson conceded, 'but don't forget this man O'Brien is new in town – and we think he might be a Skirmisher!'

That produced guffaws of laughter all round. Even fellow plotters in the cause of Irish freedom were embarrassed by O'Donovan Rossa's Skirmishers, and the Irish Republican Brotherhood were furious that these Irish Americans could so wantonly and foolishly bring the threat of reprisals down on the Irish who were living in Britain and Ireland.

The group soon grew serious again. The inept Skirmishers *had* killed a small boy and injured three people with the Salford Barracks bomb and even the more sensible Clan na Gael were turning to bombs now.

'I think my appearance *did* tell in my favour in this case,' said Best. 'That, and being half Italian. I made a deal of that. Not exactly criticizing Britain, but hinting at it.'

'Good,' said Williamson. In fact, the chief superintendent was one of the few Yard detectives who did not have foreign blood in his veins. Bilingual skills were needed by the branch, particularly as the new Extradition Act had resulted in much ferrying of prisoners across the English Channel. Even more so since so many Fenians were plotting and buying arms in Belgium and France, chiefly Paris.

They were sitting in the office of the newly formed Special Irish Branch situated in a squat little two-storey block in the centre of Scotland Yard. At least, thought Best, it was an improvement on the offices in the cramped and dingy houses that ranged around the sides of the courtyard. For a start, the windows were larger and allowed in quite a lot more light and something of a view, even if it included the gentleman's urinal situated directly below as well as the more inspiring sight of the Rising Sun public house opposite.

'He should go in one more time, I think, don't you, Dolly?' said Howard Vincent. The CID Director was the youngest and best educated man in the room and hailed from a distinctly more privileged background than the rest of them. But he and the amiable Williamson got along well enough even though Vincent had been brought in from outside to direct the newly formed CID.

'I know the editor of the *Wine Trade Gazette*,' said Vincent, who, like Best, was

25

something of a dandy with his luxuriant walrus moustache, monocle and expensive clothes courtesy of his wealthy wife. 'I'll inform him that he has a new man working for him.'

Williamson nodded. 'And I think it would be all right for Ernest to approach O'Brien this time, as he made the first move.'

And so it was.

One more time.

Harry Rice was an excitable little man with unruly hair and wild eyes that flicked about incessantly. He became particularly excited when he learned that Best was a Scotland Yard detective, stretching up towards him eagerly until he was almost teetering on his toes.

Best quietened him down a little by pretending his interest in Mary might be personal. It was better that Rice's enthusiasm was held in check, given that his ability to follow through on any offence was limited and that meanwhile he didn't want Mary to become alarmed.

Gradually, Best extracted details about Mary's living arrangements. He was not surprised to learn that she was not alone in the two second-floor rooms.

'She lives with an older man, Samuel Wickett. He seems to have plenty of money,'

Rice exclaimed. 'They live the high life. Nothing but the best.'

The incongruity of this high living conducted in low-life lodgings appeared to be lost on Rice. If Best's suspicions were correct the pair had lit on a very lucrative scheme. Probably one of several. They usually were.

'They receive a great many letters,' he told Rice, 'and what *I* would like *you* to do is to collect them after they have thrown them away.'

Rice's eyes widened.

'But I can only appoint you as my special assistant in this task,' Best went on, 'if you swear not to reveal what you are doing to anyone.'

Rice nodded eagerly. 'In return for this I will refrain from prosecuting you for the lodging-house laws you are breaking.'

Rice's eyes widened further at this and his mouth opened but Best, who now had the man in his thrall, put his finger to his lips and said, 'This is our secret. Do you understand?'

'I do. I do,' exclaimed Rice.

'I will be back when I can. It may be a while but don't doubt that I shall return.' He could hardly believe he was making these melodramatic statements, like some character in a *Strand Magazine* mystery story. 'Now I must go. Keep faith,' he ended then hur-

ried off to the Printers' Arms before he burst
out laughing.

O'Brien was safely in his place in the corner
by the fire. He hailed Best as he came in.
Best signalled back by tipping his hands
towards his mouth and raising his eyebrows.
O'Brien shook his head, indicating his half-
full glass and smiling.

When Best had his glass of Bass pale ale he
ambled over and sat down beside O'Brien as
naturally as could be. 'How's the world of
the print, Kevin?' he asked companionably.

O'Brien finished chewing his mouthful of
steak and kidney pudding and said, 'Fine.
Fine.' He paused. 'And the world of wine?'
So, he remembered Best's story. 'You don't
drink the stuff yourself, I see?'

Best grinned. 'Oh, I do, I do. But only with
food.'

O'Brien took another mouthful and considered this. 'What would you be thinking of
the American and Australian invasion?'

This was a tricky question. Obviously, he
ought to know what the man was talking
about. He considered for a moment, wrink-
ling his brow and putting his head on one
side.

'Inevitable, wasn't it with the French going
out of the picture?' He paused and smiled.
'And some of the new wines are not so bad,

despite what the French say!'

'What Australian wine would you be recommending, then?'

'Well.' Best sucked his teeth. The man's face had sharpened up considerably, he noticed. It was no longer a bland blob. 'The Ophir red, of course, though that's quite ferruginous, and the Coomaree Cabinet Burgundy has quite a nose.' He laughed. 'Down the scale a bit, the Kangaroo Port and Burgundy are passable.'

They both laughed at the cheeky New World appropriating the names of the old-world blends while placing the name of their strange national animal alongside them.

'You a wine-drinking man, Kevin?'

Clearly not one for rapid, unconsidered replies, Kevin finished off the last of his steak and kidney pudding, pushed his now empty plate to one side and said, 'I've had a glass now and then.'

When the topic changed to the latest news coming into the street, Best breathed a sigh of relief. Unfortunately, most of it concerned matters Irish and revolutionary; the execution of O'Donnell, the IRB man who had murdered James Carey, one of the Phoenix Park killers, who had turned Queen's evidence to save himself, and of Joseph Poole, who had killed a fellow Fenian suspected of being an informer. Then there was the opening of the trial of the Glasgow Ribbon-men for the gasometer explosions in January. I could not, Best decided, have picked a worse time to become friendly with O'Brien.

He trod carefully. To appear too sympathetic to the rebels might seem suspicious while the reverse attitude might well offend the man. He chose the middle ground, showing sympathy for the aims with a dash of disapproval of the methods, which was more or less how he felt anyway.

As soon as he could he edged on to safer news; a wife-murder in Plaistow and the dramatic arrival in Khartoum of the sole survivor of the massacre by the Mahdi of the ten-thousand-strong Egyptian army, led by the Englishman Hicks Pasha.

They both laughed at the idea of this sole survivor miraculously turning up, 'with a lance wound to his back'.

'I wonder which member of his family he got to do that?' laughed O'Brien.

'You can just imagine him saying, "Not too deep, not too deep",' laughed Best.

'Trouble, trouble, trouble, that's all we seem to see in the print these days,' said O'Brien, who seemed more relaxed now that Best had demonstrated knowledge of his alleged subject.

'Must get a little depressing,' sympathized Best.

'Aye, a little,' he sighed then brightened. 'But I'm going away for a break now.'

'Home for Christmas?' said Best. 'You must be pleased.'

'Well, no. Not exactly—'

Before he could continue Best broke in. 'What a coincidence. I'm going away as well.' He smiled ruefully. 'For work, unfortunately. But,' he shrugged, 'it's in Paris – so that's not so bad.'

O'Brien's hand, which had been reaching for his beer, froze halfway and he looked up, startled. Then he gathered himself and grinned. 'That's rum,' he said eventually. 'That's where I'm going!'

Best slapped his own knee and exclaimed, 'Well, I'm blowed. Would you believe it! Amazing!'

He paused, feeling it would seem quite natural to ask the man's purpose for crossing the Channel in midwinter.

He furrowed his brow. 'You got family there, Kevin?'

O'Brien shook his head. 'No. Friends.'

'Well, well,' said Best, still unable to believe the strangeness of life and its coincidences. He finished off his pint and pointed to O'Brien's glass. 'Sure I can't get you another?'

He shook his head firmly. 'I'd be off to sleep on the job and falling into the machinery, wouldn't I?'

They both laughed at the vision.

'I expect you're going to be busy while you're in Paris?' O'Brien enquired.

'Oh, yes. Yes,' nodded Best looking rueful again. 'I'll be talking to the various wine organizations. They'll all be desperate to pretend that they'll be back to normal soon.' He carefully refrained from suggesting that they meet in the French capital.

'Well,' said O'Brien, 'I hope you'll be able to spare me just a wee dram of your time.'

They both laughed again.

'I'll try,' said Best. 'I'll certainly try! When are you off?'

'Tomorrow. And you?'

'Following day.' Best picked up his pint and exclaimed, 'Santé.'

'Cheers,' said O'Brien.

'He must be suspicious,' said Cheadle. 'I know I would be.'

Best shook his head. 'I don't think so. I said about Paris before he did, remember, and I pretended I thought he was off to Ireland for Christmas.'

'Hmm,' said Cheadle. 'I dunno, I dunno.'

Neither did Best, if the truth be told.

'You could be walking into a trap.'

'Well, I don't *have* to go,' he said. 'Might even be better if I didn't.'

32

'And 'e gave you his address?'

'Well, a cafe where I could leave a message to say whether I had time to meet him.'

'One of the usual ones?'

Best nodded. The plotters made no attempt to hide their presence in Paris and they remained quite unhindered by the French authorities.

'The question is,' said Chief Inspector Littlechild, who was second-in-command of the new Special Irish Branch, 'will any purpose be served by you going there and meeting him?'

'I've no idea,' said Best who was beginning to wish he hadn't acted so rashly. Much as he loved Paris he didn't *want* to go there right now.

'Well, we know they have something big planned and we are desperate for more information, so you'd better go just in case.'

Helen was not at all amused about him going to Paris to meet a Fenian.

'They kill people, you know!' she exclaimed.

'Only by accident.'

'There's no point in joking about it Ernest! Phoenix Park wasn't an accident,' she exclaimed, tears starting into her eyes, 'and neither was the *Doterel*.'

'Actually, they think the sinking of HMS

Doterel was an accident,' he insisted, 'a gas-boiler explosion.'

The Skirmishers had claimed that they had made dynamite look like coal and had it loaded into the sloop's coal bunkers. The idea that they had at last been successful with one of their actions, killing 145 British sailors in the process, had certainly done wonders for their fund-raising and recruiting.

But there was no doubt that the Phoenix Park incident had not been an accident. The Irish Chief Secretary, Lord Frederick Cavendish, and his Permanent Under-Secretary, Thomas Burke, had been stabbed to death while walking through the Dublin park.

'Phoenix Park was claimed by the Irish Invincibles,' he said. 'Not the Fenians.'

'Nobody has heard of these Invincibles before or since! Have they? And,' her cheeks were crimson, 'let's face it, you don't *know* who *these* people are you're dealing with. Do you?'

That was true. 'But I'm not a member of the government, am I?'

'You represent it! They could be luring you there deliberately. What a coup for them – to kill one of the men sent to chase them!'

'I'll be very careful,' promised Best.

Helen said nothing but attacked her oil

painting with such ferocious brushstrokes that the canvas began to look as if it was exploding.

Five

Sited at the narrowest point in the English Channel, the port of Dover had been of strategic importance since the Roman invasion. By the time the railways loomed on the horizon, stage coaches had been rumbling along the London to Dover road for nearly two hundred years.

Given the history and importance of the route, you would think, Best ruminated peevishly, that the finest railways in Britain would take you along its seventy miles, not the worst.

There was little to choose between either of the warring railway companies who operated there. But at least the South-Eastern was beginning to improve some of its shabby rolling stock, while the London, Chatham and Dover, on which Best was travelling, still ran a motley collection of cast-offs from other companies out of the ramshackle sheds at Victoria Station which had the nerve to call itself a London railway terminus.

Thank heavens, the LCDR made at least a little more effort with their boat trains but this compartment was very small and the seats were far too upright for comfort. The only mercy was he did not have to sit on them for long. Having captured the lucrative cross-Channel mail service the LCDR made certain that their Continental expresses kept good time. In fact, they dashed along at up to forty-four miles an hour on their rickety track through crumbling tunnels and shabby stations.

Scotland Yard detectives were all too familiar with this dreary route but at least, on this occasion, Best did not have to traverse it twice in one day, as they were obliged to do when escorting extradited prisoners to France. On these occasions they departed Victoria Station at dawn, reached Calais by midday, delivered the prisoner to the French police then returned by the same boat. To think some police officers envied the Yard men their 'foreign travel'!

To take his mind off of being jolted and jarred in his too-upright seat Best dug into his portmanteau and took out a small packet of crumpled and torn letters.

The previous day he had returned to the

Printers' Arms as usual, even though he knew that O'Brien had already left for Paris. There was always the chance that one of his pals might check out whether he had turned up. Even the Skirmishers were becoming more careful these days. On the way, he had called in on the excitable Mr Rice at his Craven Buildings establishment. The landlord had been busy on Best's behalf.

'I had to search through a lot of rubbish to find them,' said Rice, eyes wide and neck stretching upwards as he handed over the bundle of letters. 'Some was just too disgusting, covered in rancid food and Heaven knows what else. Thought you wouldn't want those.' He was right there.

His place was looking cleaner and tidier, Best noticed, and his register, doubtless rapidly brought up to date and generally tinkered with, was prominent on the battered kitchen table which passed for his office desk.

In fact Rice's establishment was not the kind for which the Common Lodging Houses Act of 1851 had been passed and regularly amended. These had dirty, crowded and lice-ridden dormitories that were dens of vice and crime. Nonetheless, Rice's rooms must be liable to *some* laws and some of these would be being broken. Best had no idea which ones. Rice probably didn't either.

37

The letters Rice had so assiduously gathered for Best expressed much sympathy with poor G.C., some of them at great length. They expressed the hope that 'F' would come to his senses and do the right thing by her – if only in remembrance of their 'happy past'. They begged her not to lose faith and to remember that life could get better – particularly, some claimed, if she embraced the Lord.

'Meanwhile', several of the correspondents added, here was 'a small token', 'a little relief to tide you over' or 'a contribution in the name of charity'. Some letters actually mentioned the amount enclosed, which ranged from a few shillings to several pounds. Two of the writers wanted to meet poor G.C. in order that they might get to know this homeless, friendless and ill lady better and judge how they could help her further.

Interesting how they all presumed that the writer was a woman and how excited they were by the idea of her being friendless and alone.

Since this was only a fraction of their takings, G.C. and her male friend had clearly devised a cunning scheme. How clever of them to send out an agonized call for help addressed, not to the public, but to a particular, apparently heartless man – as though unaware that the hearts of many other readers might be touched.

Best had seen many varieties of the fraudulent newspaper advertisement, but this was one of the cleverest.

Six

Best blinked at the bright light as the train emerged from the last of a series of tunnels which burrowed through chalk hills to reach Dover Harbour Station.

When his eyes grew accustomed to the light he glanced up at the soaring cliffs to his left on top of which stood that powerful defensive fortress, Dover Castle.

This superbly positioned 'Key to England' was a splendid sight, a massive square-hewn Norman keep astride a high mound, protected by two walls and bristling with watchtowers, barbicans and bulwarks. Impregnable, it would seem. But within the inner bailey stood a stark reminder that Britain's defences had in fact been breached well before the Normans came: the ruins of a Roman lighthouse.

The Harbour Station was close to the

seafront and to Admiralty Pier, where their ferry awaited. The train negotiated the short, sharply curved link from the station to the pier then began to trundle out above the unfriendly waves – a strangely unsettling experience.

It soon idled to a halt but the passengers were obliged to wait in the carriages or shiver on the tiny platform until the Post Office vans were opened and stooped figures had finished carrying mail bags across the railway track to the ferry. Nothing was more important than the mail.

The silence was broken only by the screams of the seagulls and the sound of the waves slapping angrily against the parapet behind them.

It could have been worse. Best had seen the waves wash over and half-drown the passengers. Even so ... He stared out at the leaden skies and dark, choppy seas and shivered. It was cold, damp and horrible out there. Why, he wondered again, did I tell O'Brien that I was going to Paris! The Channel crossing could be such a miserable experience, particularly at this bleak time of year.

The mail exchange completed, passengers were now shepherded across the line. Several tried to open their umbrellas in an attempt to protect themselves from the sea spray which whirled around them. Others held on to their hats. Some attempted to do both and ended up not only damp and bedraggled but frustrated as well.

Ze mad Anglaise, who sported 'fore-and-aft caps', could now afford to look smug. These had peaks both back and front and ear flaps which were normally tied on top of the head but for Channel crossings were fastened securely under their chins.

Some German passengers had adopted a different approach to surviving the rigours of a Channel crossing in winter. They wore immense fur coats, boots and hats, but while they did not shiver like some of the others, the extra bulk and weight caused them to stagger in an ungainly fashion when it came to navigating the gangway.

The twin-hulled paddle steamer, *Calais–Douvres*, puffed away impatiently as these assorted windswept passengers made their unsteady way aboard. It was a curious sight, each hull having its own tall, slim funnels and alternate small Tricolours and Union Jacks at each prow and stern. Flapping wildly at the corners of the saloon were the larger Blue Ensign and the flag of the London, Chatham and Dover Railway.

The idea of cobbling two ships together in the hope that they'd prove more stable than one alone appealed to Best's sense of the ridiculous. At least it was one of the newer, bigger designs. The older, smaller craft were tossed about horribly in bad weather.

Best was neither a bad sailor nor a good one but somewhere in between. Sometimes he was sick, very sick, sometimes not. Of course, this depended upon how smooth or rough the crossing. Judging by the swell that was raising and lowering the *Calais–Douvres* today's journey did not look promising.

At least, he comforted himself, he didn't have to cross twice this time, one way with a prisoner in tow. Keeping an eye on a prisoner whilst one or both of you were being sick was neither an easy nor a pleasant task.

'She's quite a vessel, isn't she?' said a voice to his left. It was an American voice. A Southern American voice. 'Or should I say, *two* vessels. Two ships tied together! My, my, ain't that something.'

Best turned to see a tall, well-set gentleman hanging on to a grey felt slouch hat which the fitfully gusting wind was threatening to carry away. Not surprising, thought Best. It *was* a rather splendid hat, with a wide brim edged with darker grey and a broad matching ribbon encircling the crown.

The lively, animated face beneath sported chestnut-brown side-whiskers, a close-trimmed moustache and dark brown eyes that had a humorous glint. His Inverness overcoat was open and Best noticed that his free thumb was resting in the pocket of his pearl-grey silk waistcoat – a *double-breasted* waist-coat.

The security people in Dublin had warned them that one sure way of picking out an American citizen was by their square-toed shoes, double-breasted waistcoats and felt hats. Not that there was any doubt in this case.

'Twin hulls are one of the ways they are testing to try to make the crossing smooth-er,' smiled Best.

'And does it?'

Best grinned. 'Not that I've noticed.'

'Oh, dear.'

Best laughed. 'But they persist in trying. This is the second twin hull and they gave another boat a tilting saloon deck which was meant to stay level whatever the weather.'

'And that didn't work either?' enquired the Southern gentleman.

Best shook his head. 'It was a disaster.' He laughed again. 'For some reason it kept bumping into Calais harbour. Mind you, nearly all the big ships did that sometimes.'

'Oh, dear.' The man glanced at the long prows of the *Calais–Douvres*.

'Oh, it's all right now,' Best assured him. 'They've improved Calais harbour. Had to, before it was reduced to rubble!'

'Well, sir, that's one relief, I guess. And we must give them full marks for trying.' The man paused. 'You sound as if you are a regular traveller?'

'Oh, no.' Best shrugged and said carefully, 'I just go over now and then on holiday or for business.'

'And what if I may enquire, is your...'

To Best's relief at that moment it was their turn to board. He stood aside with a great show of manners to allow the American gentleman to precede him onto the gangway.

Had this man made friends with him to avoid the notice of the port police, who were on the supposedly discreet lookout for Irish or Irish-American travellers? Several Metropolitan Police detectives had been drafted down here for that purpose.

Best recognized one of them lurking by the top of the gangway, doing a poor job of looking inconspicuous himself. At least he had the sense not to acknowledge him. They were there primarily to watch for incoming Fenians and to signal customs officers waiting on the platform that they should give a suspect's luggage another search.

If his new acquaintance *was* a Fenian he must know that Americans were instantly recognizable by the cut of their clothes, not to mention the shape of their whiskers. This one did seem to be out of the usual Fenian

mould. Were not most of them from Northern cities?

If the man *was* a Fenian he might well have
been charged with finding out more about
Best. I must be vigilant, Best thought. I don't
want to suffer the fate of James Carey. Carey
was one of the Phoenix Park killers; he had
turned informer to save himself but was
murdered just as the ship carrying him to
safety in South Africa had almost reached
Cape Town. Would a Scotland Yard detective
attempting to infiltrate their organization
prove as tempting a target? He thought they
might. Helen was sure they would. There
had been a time when to die would not have
seemed so terrible. A relief, almost. But he
was happy now with Helen and Lucy Jane.

Once on board, Best tucked himself away
in one of the small private cabins on the
inside of the farthest hull and settled down
to reading the latest copy of the *Wine Trade
Gazette*. He must bring himself up to date on
the current situation in the French vineyards
and learn more about wine in general.

When he had arrived home with the
ridiculous news that he was now a wine
expert and was going, of all places, to Paris
in that guise, Helen had rushed about looking for the Victoria Wine Company's latest
sales leaflet. From this, he had culled the
names of the Californian and Australian

wines he had so glibly quoted to O'Brien. But now he was going to the land of wine and the names of despised New World wines would not be much help to him there.

The sheer folly of his pretence came home to him as he struggled to assimilate the latest news and at the same time to ignore the disturbing movement of the ship.

He was distracted by the thunderous roar of the paddles which sat between the two hulls. His glance kept drifting out of the window to watch the water rushing and pounding through them. What was it about moving water, he wondered, that so drew your eye and kept you idly watching? But it was wine, not water, he should be concentrating on!

It was no good. He gave up. He couldn't concentrate and keep a settled stomach. Reading increased the threat of seasickness. He needed food. He would have to rely on his wit and native cunning to get him through the French wine jungle.

Fortunately, by the time he made his unsteady way to the saloon, the sea had calmed somewhat, but remained unrelentingly sombre. The saloon was only half full and there was a tentative air among the passengers who lined the red-plush banquet seats and sat around the circular mahogany tables. Some took occasional glances out of the windows and reported back to their companions, who were clearly hoping their luck was going to hold and that the waves would not grow larger.

Best took in the situation in a sweeping glance but was careful not to let his eye settle anywhere in case they met those of the American gentleman. But no sooner was he seated with his glass of Allsopp's Ale and a large beef and horseradish sandwich than he sensed a large presence looming over him.

'Hello! There you are!' exclaimed the jovial Southern gentleman. 'I've been looking for you.'

How direct. How American. For once, he thought, I would have been glad of some of that dispiriting English reserve.

But he looked up, smiled politely and said, 'Please join me.' If the man is going to try to kill me I might as well make his acquaintance first, he thought dourly.

'George R. Hardinge,' the American said as he sat down and held out his hand, 'from Georgia.'

Best took it and said quietly, 'Halliday, Ernest Halliday.'

'Don't let me disturb your repast,' said George R., pointing at Best's plate.

'Oh, you won't,' said Best. He picked up the sandwich and grinned. 'I'm going to let you do all the talking!'

George R. laughed heartily. 'My pleasure, sir. My pleasure.'

'You can tell me what you are doing crossing the English Channel at this godforsaken time of the year when, I presume, you might be enjoying a kinder climate on dry land back home?'

This direct but decorous speech was catching, thought Best as he bit into his sandwich. With luck, George R.'s reply would continue until they reached Calais, which, by his reckoning, was only twenty minutes away. The *Calais–Douvres* was the fastest Channel steamer yet, making the crossing in only an hour and a half.

'Well, sir,' said George R. as he slowly removed his chamois-leather gloves and placed them tidily one above the other on the table beside him, 'it's all on account of Isabella and her compatriots.' He twinkled. 'And a little bit of graft I'm engaged in.'

Best stopped chewing and gazed at him. Isabella? Isabella? The name was familiar. Where had he heard it recently?

George R. watched him with an amused expression, twisting the square-cut diamond ring on his left forefinger around and around as he did so.

Best began to chew again. Not heard it, read it. He finished his mouthful, swallowed and held up a finger. 'The lady is a vine.'

George R. slapped the table. 'Correct, correct. My, my, you are a well-informed fellow, Ernest.'

Best tipped his head to one side self-deprecatingly and took a swig of beer, determined to say as little as possible.

'Isabella,' revealed George R., hoping he wasn't telling Ernest something he already knew, 'is one of the guilty parties. The causes of all this misery that is blighting Europe and, particularly, of course, la Belle France.'

Seven

The sun struggled out for Best's first morning in Paris, which cheered him somewhat as he left his pension in the Boulevard Saint-Germain. He had chosen to stay among the government institutions and university colleges in the hope of avoiding both Fenians and their Scotland Yard watchers.

Fortunately that was not difficult. The revolutionaries made no secret of their whereabouts and had proved to be creatures of habit. It appeared that they felt little need to hide themselves. Indeed, it sometimes seemed as if they wanted to make sure the British police knew where to find them: at the Café du Rond Point near the Arc de Triomphe, the English and American Bar on the Rue Royale (kept by a Fenian) and even the Irish Club by the Champ de Mars.

As Best made his way along the bank of the Seine to the Quai d'Orsay the early morning sun lit up the river and reflected onto the windows of the newly restored Palais de la Legion d'Honneur, which had been so badly damaged by the Commune in 1871. However, the once fine Palais du Conseil d'Etat was a sad sight, still gaunt and blackened from their incendiary fires.

Best hoped that London would not have to suffer like this despite all the reported Fenian threats to destroy the Tower of London, the Houses of Parliament and even Scotland Yard. Some policemen were of the opinion that a bomb was just what the Yard needed, as long it was empty at the time. At least they might get some decent offices when it was rebuilt.

He turned south into the Rue du Bac then right into the Rue de Grenelle where he found what he was seeking; the premises of the Société d'Agriculture. If anyone was watching him he had better be seen to be doing what he had claimed to be doing – reporting on the latest chapter in the wine-trade tragedy.

According to what he had learned it was this society and the *Journal d'Agriculture Practique* which, in 1868, had first reported the disturbing news that the leaves of vines in Pujaut in the Vaucluse had become stunted and sick and that the grapes were beginning to die. It seemed that it made no difference whether the vines were old or new or in what type of soil they were planted – the tiny pale yellow aphids had marched on across the region like an army of soldier ants. Travelling above and below ground they sucked the life out of the leaves and vine roots, leaving them blackened and crumbling, and reproducing themselves at an alarming rate as they went.

'In the same year,' said Gaston Verone, a wine expert seated opposite him in a tiny, high-ceilinged office, 'the Americans sent a special commission to see what they could learn from us about wine production.' He laughed. 'These gentlemen were not pleased, I think, that their wines were awarded zero in the wine-tastings at our Exposition Universelle!'

Best smiled but said nothing, hoping he would continue addressing him as though he was totally ignorant on the subject.

Verone took his silence as a criticism. He lifted his shoulders, extended his hands, raised his eyebrows and pursed his lips in typically Gallic fashion.

'They were not to our European taste. They were too, how shall we say, musky, foxy, raspberry-flavoured.' He grinned again. 'We called them *pissat de renard*.'

That must have pleased their guests, thought Best, to have their choicest wines likened to fox's piss.

'They imagined that Ohio was going to become the Rhine of America and Georgia their Beaujolais!' He chuckled.

'Their wine came from their native vines, didn't it?' said Best, who thought it time he offered some informed comment as well as halting the unpleasant triumphalism from this puffed-up little man. 'Of course now we know *why* they weren't able to keep their European vines alive over there, don't we?'

Verone gazed at him silently from under his beetle brows. Eventually he said, *'Absolument.'* He sighed and nodded. 'Now we know. Now we know.' He passed his hand over his wiry black hair in a gesture of despair, let it drop to the end of his stiffly straight moustache and kept it there, fingering it, as he proclaimed morosely, 'It's a tragedy for France. A tragedy.'

It was also a developing disaster for Spain, Germany, Portugal, Hungary, Austria, Serbia and Slovenia, but Best remained silent about that.

Next, Best went to the French Ministry of Agriculture, which initially had shown little interest in the tiny yellow aphid that had since been christened by the experts as *Phylloxera vastatrix* – dry leaf devastator. Now they were not just interested in it but obsessed by it – as was all of France.

Their spokesman, M. de Marcellin, a pleasant, harassed-looking individual with crooked front teeth and wispy hair, was charged with persuading the world that their wine trade was not dead. He reminded Best that France was home to almost half the world's vineyards; six million farmers had been engaged in cultivating their matchless vines and two million more were employed in the peripheral trades manufacturing bottles, corks and labels, transporting and storing the finished product and, finally, selling it.

Then he admitted to what was undeniable, that a million hectares of vineyards had been destroyed and 664,000 more were infested with the tiny, deadly aphid, phylloxera, and that this was, indeed, a national disaster.

'But,' de Marcellin sat up straighter and did his best to inject hope into his voice, 'we are fighting back and *we will win*!'

There wasn't much else he *could* say. Best felt sorry for this nice little man. He enquired politely about the current situation in the war between the sulphurists and the Americanists.

'There is a – rapprochement,' de Marcellin assured him.

Impasse was what Best had heard.

'They are beginning to realize,' he continued, 'that both methods – in conjunction – hold out hope and that, together, they will triumph!'

What Best had read was that the sulphurists insisted that only by drenching the vines with sulphur insecticide, which had helped quell oïdium, an earlier fungal infection, could they halt the scourge, and that this spraying was government-subsidized. That they held sway on the Commission Supérieure du Phylloxera and seemed keen to not only ignore the reported good results achieved by the Americanists, who grafted French vines onto phylloxera-resistant American vine roots, but also, it was rumoured, even tampered with the figures so they read in favour of sulphurism.

He knew that the Americanists held that since it was on the American vines that the unwelcome visitors had arrived in Europe, most of these vines were themselves immune to their depredations. Therefore, it was a good idea to graft French vines onto their roots, an idea that had horrified many

Frenchmen.

Now, in desperation, many were trying the method. But the three-year gap in production this entailed plus the increasing price of the American vines made the method untenable for the poorer farmers. The Americanists insisted that Reconstitution, as it was called, should *also* be supported by the government. Despite the opposition, the grafting idea was gaining more and more supporters but (according to the *Wine Trade Gazette*) the price of American vines was subject to some cynical profiteering. It was ever thus.

Best mentioned none of this to the hard-pressed M. Marcellin, who now announced brightly, 'We are still receiving many interesting entries to our competition for a practical remedy.'

Best had read about some of these suggestions. Indeed, they had become something of a national joke, giving rise to ribald cartoons in the French press and the labelling of some contestants as *fantaisistes*. Not surprisingly, among the more sensible ideas came others more outré, such as coating the roots with snail secretions, drowning them in human urine (male only, of course) and blasting them with bolts from that newest of discoveries, electricity.

But Best did not want to embarrass this

man so he nodded, looked impressed and took notes. He even forbore to mention the burgeoning trade in spurious substitutes made of dried raisins or sugar and dye. After all, he was not here for that purpose.

Duty done and, hopefully, any Fenian watchers deceived, Best decided to take a chance and cross the Seine in search of Le Chat Noir, the restaurant in Montmartre where O'Brien had promised to leave him a message.

It again struck Best what a manic venture this was. The restaurant could well be another Fenian haunt and O'Brien might even turn up with some of his more lethal colleagues. He sighed. Well, there was nothing for it now but to plough on.

He began looking for an omnibus station. There was no leaping out and stopping a bus like you did in London. Paris omnibuses were strictly and, he had to confess, admirably well-regulated. Though that did make the whole business rather long-winded.

He found an omnibus station or bureau in the Rue du Bac and gave the birdlike little ticket seller his destination, Boulevard Bonne Nouvelle. He was duly issued with a numbered ticket, instructed to change at Madeleine and told to wait in turn for the Vaugirard–St-Lazare omnibus which was, lest he could not read French quickly enough, white with one green and one red lamp.

When the 'bus arrived the driver called out the numbers and boarding took place in strict rotation. By the time it was Best's turn there was only one seat left, and he was relieved to see that it was inside. Riding outside was cheaper but jolting along on top for all of Paris to see was not the best way to conceal one's presence in the capital. Besides, it got chilly up there at this time of year.

He located the restaurant down a narrow alleyway not far from the Boulevard Bonne Nouvelle. The outside of Le Chat Noir was faded and uninspiring with flaking green paintwork, a sun-bleached menu and an interior well hidden behind long and heavy curtains. There was an almost uninhabited air about the place.

Inside, too, there had been little attempt to provide anything but the plainest décor and the simplest of tables and chairs. The walls were lined with pictures featuring black cats but they had a forlorn air. It was as if some-one had put them there many years before in a fit of enthusiasm for a new venture but since then had lost interest in them. The cats ranged from the sweet and playful, *avec* balls of wool, to slant-eyed and sinister witches' familiars.

Beside the till sat another black cat; a large marble one wearing an aloof expression as if its feline dignity had been affronted by the notices hung about its neck, one giving the opening times, the other advising customers not to ask for credit.

An impatient waiter thumbed through a clip of messages that lay beside the large black cat. Obviously this was a place of assignments. Finally he stopped his flicking, selected a note from near the bottom and handed it to Best with one hand while reaching for a brandy bottle with the other.

A meeting was possible, Best learned. Indeed, O'Brien had chosen that very evening at 7.30 p.m., in that very café. So soon. Best was surprised.

He was also relieved. Perhaps, if the meeting came to nothing – and he couldn't really see what could be gained – he could go home tomorrow.

Might it be that the man really was in Paris to meet friends? That he was not a Fenian after all? They had made mistakes about that before.

Eight

I'm being foolishly optimistic, Best thought. To discover whether his optimism was justified he went into a telegraph office on the Boulevard des Capucines and enquired whether there might be a telegram for Mr Ernest Halliday.

There was. The contents were not encouraging. 'Consultations with Rogers, Jones and Rawlinson have taken place and gone well', it read.

Oh dear. O'Brien was a Fenian. It looked like he wouldn't be going home tomorrow after all.

Fenian was rather a loose term for the various Irish freedom fighters who had gathered in Paris during the last few years. The Fenian Brotherhood, founded in 1858, had gained members and arms expertise during the American Civil War, when Irishmen fought on both sides. The Fenians soon split into two groups and later the Clan na Gael was founded. Between them they organized two attempted invasions of Canada and alongside the Dublin-based Irish Revolutionary Brotherhood (IRB) two failed attempts at uprisings in Ireland.

Best recalled when their fight came to England fifteen years ago when he joined the police. Three IRB members were arrested while attempting to raid the Chester Castle arsenal but two escaped after a daring rescue from a Manchester prison van planned by a leading Fenian, Richard O'Sullivan Burke. In the process a police sergeant had been shot dead – accidentally it was claimed.

This single act had led into a downward spiral of tragedy, each act, as in a Greek tragedy, leading on to another more terrible. Three of the men convicted of the Manchester rescue were hanged. They became the Manchester Martyrs. Burke was later caught and interned in the Middlesex House of Detention in Clerkenwell.

In this instance a prison-van rescue was judged too difficult given the heavy police guard and the state of the traffic-choked London roads. Instead, IRB members placed a barrel containing two hundred pounds of gunpowder against the wall of the prison exercise yard. The signal to Burke that he should keep clear and be ready to run was a white rubber ball thrown over the wall just before detonation. The resulting huge explosion achieved its aim, in that it demolished a large section of the prison wall. Unfortunately, it also devastated many of the houses opposite, killing thirteen people and injuring a great many more. Ironically, Burke had been unable to take advantage of this effort on his behalf. He was locked up in his cell at the time, an informer having revealed that an escape attempt was planned. Had police surveillance been better the tragedy might never have occurred.

And so it went on. In turn the Clerkenwell bombers were caught. One of them, Michael Barrett, was hanged – the last man in England to be publicly executed.

In 1871 after a long lull when Fenian activity was judged spent an amnesty on condition of exile was granted to five IRB men convicted of treason-felony for planning the 1865 uprising in Ireland. The released men, who included Jeremiah O'Donovan Rossa, went to the USA, where they promptly became involved in much more ambitious plans.

On the agenda were a bigger and better uprising in Ireland, the development of a tiny submarine capable of attacking British shipping and the bombing of Britain, but there was disagreement as to how these aims should be achieved. O'Donovan Rossa thought the fight should be brought to the heart of the enemy and set up a skirmishing fund. The Salford bombing and all the early attacks in Glasgow, Manchester and London were the work of Skirmishers, much to the embarrassment of the IRB and the Clan; but the Clan themselves eventually turned to dynamite, which led to a split with the IRB. All came and went in Paris, where the American Land League deposited huge sums collected for the relief of evicted tenants in Ireland, a great deal of which was diverted by the Clan.

But the name Fenian stuck and was used loosely to cover all.

When he caught the delicious aromas drifting from the kitchen of Le Chat Noir, Best realized that he'd been wrong about dining there being an unpromising prospect. This was obviously one of those places confident enough in its food and custom not to bother about anything else.

He relaxed. Even though O'Brien was a Fenian and the long curtains shut out the outside world they weren't going to try to kill him here. Anything could happen, unnoticed here, but, he was sure, the French were too civilized to allow any interference with a good meal.

Even slight acquaintances quickly become friends when they are a long way from home and are usually greeted as such even if they haven't much in common. So it was with O'Brien and Best.

The Irishman approached Best, his face alight with pleasure. 'Ernest! Glad you could come!' He held out his chunky, calloused hand in greeting.

Best wondered why he had ever imagined that the man's face was bland. O'Brien was one of those people whose faces are closed off in repose but in conversation open like a flower responding to the sun.

He was a nice man, Best soon decided. He was friendly, pleasant company and could tell a good tale, as was expected of an Irishman. But all the time O'Brien was regaling him with his stories about the strange people he had met since his arrival (the French), Best kept in mind that the man had also been in company with three of the more fiery Fenians: the Casey brothers and Eugene Davis.

Patrick Casey had been one of the Clerkenwell bombers and Joseph had been with Burke when he was arrested for the Manchester rescue. Like O'Brien both the Casey brothers were newspaper compositors, while Eugene Davis was the Paris correspondent for the *United Irishman*, Rossa's rabid publication which had helped him become dubbed wearily by fellow Fenians as Jeremiah

O'Dynamite. The telegram Best received earlier had confirmed that O'Brien had met all three since his arrival in Paris.

The food proved as delicious as the aromas promised. In lulls between mouthfuls of delicious vichyssoise and bites of succulent beef chasseur and potatoes Anna, Best took his turn with a few anecdotes of his own. He made O'Brien smile over the sadly optimistic official at the Ministry of Agriculture who tried to persuade him that all would be well and that a Gallic victory would soon be wrought over this filthy foreign insect.

Another character taking a bow in their conversation was George R. Hardinge, who had informed him that only by grafting French vines onto the despised American vine roots would they be saved and that the French wine community was divided between the pro-grafters and the non-grafters.

As the wine flowed Best noticed that O'Brien was gradually becoming quieter, more serious – and also somewhat nervous. He kept glancing towards the door and trying to see between the curtains as if he was expecting someone to come in or something to happen.

Best knew that to thwart British government informers the Fenians had not only reduced the number of people involved in making their 'war plans' but had also decided that any informers caught were to be summarily dealt with. But then O'Brien wasn't divulging any secrets, was he? Maybe he was still wary of Best? Or maybe they had discovered that he was a police detective and were planning to eliminate him?

Gradually they both began to get a little tight. Best was usually a quietly happy drunk, all his worries dropping away and being replaced by a warm glow. On this occasion, he was kept alert by those glances at the door and O'Brien's insistent plying of him with a wine made expensive by the predations of those evil aphids.

The alcohol made him uncharacteristically indecisive. If he got out now he would save his life but possibly ruin a vital exchange which might save other people's lives. His instincts told him he should leave but O'Brien was becoming maudlin and he seemed to want to tell him something. He kept leaning forward, gazing at him intently, a worried frown on his face and an anxious look in his eye. He would open his mouth, rock a little in his chair, then close it again.

Best was still transfixed by his dilemma when his new Irish friend leaned over suddenly, grabbed Best's right sleeve and said, 'What would you do, Ernest,' he said pleadingly, 'what would you do, if you knew about something terrible, something that might kill or injure innocent people, but knew that if you reported it you would betray friends?' He was gabbling now. 'Might cost them, cost them – ' there were tears in his eyes – 'their freedom or ... or – ' he found it hard to get out something which had been weighing so heavily on his mind – 'their lives?'

Nine

Best was greatly relieved when the fort at the end of Dover's Admiralty Pier came into view; the wintry sun glinting off the eighty-ton guns trained seaward in the hope of repulsing potential invaders.

He was relieved not only because he had managed to keep seasickness at bay, the return crossing having been rougher than the outward, but also because he would soon be back on home ground where he felt safer.

The only disturbing factor was the pre-sence of the man sitting opposite him in one of the well-padded booths of the *Calais–Douvres* saloon.

Best had been congratulating himself on his escape from the possibly lethal clutches of the Irish Americans in Paris when, just as he was about to board the home-bound ferry, he heard his name being called. He recognized the voice immediately. The deep, languid tones of the American South were not often heard on the Channel crossing during the winter. He turned to see George R. Hardinge, one hand gripping the gangway rail, the other holding aloft his splendid grey felt slouch hat.

The Scotland Yard man instantly wondered whether it could really be a coincidence that they had both finished their business in France at the same time. Or, as he had originally suspected, was George R. a Fenian who was following him? Were they letting him know that they had identified him and were laying in wait?

He hoped to Heaven that O'Brien was all right. That the nervousness which had kept the man's glance straying towards the restaurant door in Montmartre had not proved justified.

But why should George R. Hardinge, an obviously prosperous, probably Protestant, Southern gentleman, be a Fenian? Most of their strongholds were in the north: Boston, Chicago, Philadelphia and New York. Did the man feel sympathy with the Irish wanting their freedom from the English as had *they* from the Union? Was that it? A freedom, of course, which they had been loath to grant to their own black slaves or the American Indian. Could people be so perverse and hypocritical? Best wondered before answering his own question. Of course they could.

Maybe George R. become fired up by his Irish comrades in the US Civil War? Or maybe he just had a personal score to settle with the British? Or then again perhaps he was just what he said he was – someone who had gone to France to help the French with their wine problems?

He put all of these doubts and questions to the back of his mind as they settled down in the saloon, Best with his tea and plain biscuits, which were all his stomach could tolerate at the moment, George R. with his tumbler of whisky.

The ship was too small and the journey too short for division of the classes so they were mixed in a manner unlikely to be found elsewhere. Only those unable to find the extra two shillings for entry were left outside on deck. Inside were young milords returning from their European tours in time for their Christmas house parties and New Year hunts, wealthy mamas and daughters sated by their expenditure in Paris fashion houses, frowning businessmen consulting their accounts, home-bound sailors – and desperate French farmers anxious to make some money from their other produce now that their vineyards had died.

Several passengers glanced up sharply when they heard George R.'s Southern drawl. Some watched him for a while, absorbing the unusual cut of his jacket, his fancy grey silk waistcoat and his gold cravat and dazzled by his captivating and expansive manner. Eventually, their attention had drifted away, their faces acquiring the trance-like expressions of the long-distance traveller suspended in time, waiting for it to pass so that they can begin their lives again.

One toddler in a sailor suit remained beguiled by the exotic sight and sound until his parents insisted that he stop staring so rudely at the gentleman. Best noticed that the attention of two other passengers seemed to keep drifting back to George R. Hardinge. Shabbily dressed middle-aged men who sat on the other side of the saloon. One was otherwise wrapped in his thoughts most of the time but the second kept shifting about on his seat and agitatedly fiddling with his large battered clay pipe; one of those French pipes with a bowl in the shape of a human head. The man filled the pipe, tamped the tobacco down and was about to light it when the first man leaned over and said something to him and he got up and went outside.

Best had begun their conversation by enquiring how George R. had got on with the French wine bureaucrats, feeling it wise to keep learning about the subject before revealing that he, too, had been in Paris on wine business.

'The real problem, sir,' said George R. thoughtfully stroking his luxurious side-whiskers then pulling at the ends as his hand reached them, 'is that the French think we Americans are idiots. That we are plumb ignorant when it comes to food and wine – and most other things too, come to that. Which is why for years they sent us all their barrel scrapings and gave them the name of some fancy vintage. For this reason also, as well as for the sake of national pride, some are now still reluctant to accept our assistance – and our pest-free vines. They are suspicious of our motives – added to which they blame us for the grape-vine louse in the first place.'

Best laughed. 'Not so well, then. If it's any consolation they're not very impressed by us, either! They call us Perfidious Albion – so we are deceitful and treacherous as well as being stupid.'

'Oh, well,' George R. drawled, '*we* ain't so bad, then. That's a relief!'

They both laughed warmly.

'To a foolish brotherhood,' said Best, holding up his fleurs-de-lis teacup.

George R. responded by tilting his whisky tumbler. 'I guess we'll just have to survive without their approval!' He fished out his watch, a large gold triple-calendar hunter, flicked it open, glanced at the white enamel dial, closed it and replaced it in his waistcoat pocket. The cover of this timepiece was embellished with a blue-and-white enamel crest made up of four white plumes clasped together by a blue-and-gold-lettered strap.

Best noticed all of this because that was the fourth time George R. had looked at his watch. Was he meeting someone at Dover and worried that he might be late? As far as he knew the ferry was running on time.

He had also been glancing towards the saloon door at intervals and around at his fellow travellers. It was uncanny that so much of his behaviour resembled that of O'Brien last night. Was George R. also about to confess all? Or was he merely keeping an eye open for a co-conspirator?

The American's conversation betrayed no anxiety, however, merely continued on in its warm and jovial fashion. But then he was a more educated, privileged and cultured man than O'Brien and as such probably made it a habit of not betraying his real feelings lest they be taken for weakness or bad form.

As it transpired, Best was not obliged to conjure up some excuse to learn about George R.'s involvement in the US Civil War. The subject evolved naturally from their conversation regarding the recovery of Paris after the Franco-Prussian War and the siege of the capital twelve years earlier. This enabled him to enquire about the South's own reconstruction problems following their Civil War.

'Let us say they are still in a state of flux,' George R. replied laconically. 'We've recovered from the Black Terror and the Federal troops are gone at last but...' He shrugged and spread his hands to indicate 'not good'. 'Carpet-bagging, corruption, poverty.'

'Inevitable, I suppose,' said Best shaking his head in sympathy. He was reluctant to enquire about the man's part in the war or where his sympathies had actually lain. But George R. gave him a long look and said in his straightforward American way, 'I guess you're wondering what I did then?' He gave a half-smile. 'It isn't only the Northerners who were Old Abolitionists, you know,' he said, referring to those US citizens who favoured the abolition of slavery before the Civil War began. 'Some of *us* were also. But that didn't stop me fighting alongside my neighbours. They invaded us, by God!'

'It must have been terrible.'

'Horrific. Civil war is something to be avoided at all costs.' George R. contemplated that thought solemnly for a while then brightened. 'But that is where the vine came in. The cotton trade was devastated but our native vines began to flourish and give hope to some of us in Missouri, South Carolina and Georgia. That's why it's a privilege to offer them in the cause of saving France,' he grinned, 'since they helped us rout the British in our revolution.'

Best smiled. Ah, that gave some hint of where his loyalties lay.

'The trouble is,' laughed George R., 'now it's not only our black brethren who are seeking emancipation. One movement has sparked off another.'

Best was puzzled. 'Trouble is'? He didn't think Fenianism was a good thing? Then it dawned on him. 'Anna Dickinson and Susan B. Anthony?' he said, naming two Boston campaigners for the rights of women. Ironically, Helen had informed him, it had been the exclusion of women from a World Anti-Slavery Convention in London back in 1840 which had given *their* fight its impetus.

'You *are* informed, my friend.'

Best grinned. 'No, my wife is. Your ladies have infected ours much like your phylloxera has infected the French vines.'

'Oh, dear.'

So as not to offend the man, Best began talking about the long struggle for freedom of his mother's country, Italy, and amused him by relating how angry the French had been when the Italian revolutionary Orsini had plotted his assassination attempt on Napoleon III in the safety of London. They shook their heads at the madness of the world and wondered when justice and equality for all would prevail.

Best had decided that George R. made an agreeable and entertaining companion on a tedious journey. He had that engagingly friendly and optimistic outlook which sometimes made Europeans appear depressingly jaded. This time he was tempted *not* to find ways to avoid being trapped in a train carriage with him on the way to London, as he had done on the outward journey from Calais to Paris.

He had done this partly so that his real identity would not be accidentally revealed in a moment of bonhomie or his ignorance about wine, his supposed reason for visiting the French capital, exposed. He had also borne in mind the dangerous darkness of the long train tunnels en route. More than one railway murderer had taken advantage of the fact that his fellow traveller was blinded when thrown into the sudden acridly smoky blackness.

Such a notion seemed ridiculous now as Best glanced at the jovial man sitting across from him. But common sense prevailed nonetheless. The man had not really revealed his true self yet. He would make the train journey back to London alone, just to be on the safe side. So, how would he do that?

The easiest excuse he decided was merely to point out that he was travelling in second class (the Receiver would not countenance paying for first). He imagined that this obviously wealthy American gentleman would be reclining on one of the padded first-class armchairs which helped deaden the rattle and cushion the jerky movement of LCDR's aptly named rolling stock, and elevating his feet on one of their extending footrests. The difficulty with this excuse was that George might offer to suffer second class for the sake of Best's company or pay the difference for his.

In the event he found he had wasted his mental energy. As soon as the ship began drawing alongside Admiralty Pier once more George R. stood up, shook Best's hand heartily, declared how much he had enjoyed his company and urged him to 'come visit' him some day.

Ten

As always after a journey abroad Best found himself gazing at the English countryside with renewed appreciation. It amused him to try to see it almost with the eyes of a recently arrived foreigner.

The rolling chalk hills of Kent with their alternating pastureland and woodland still looked lovely even in the fading afternoon light of winter.

He had now seen the Garden of England in all its guises; its orchards a sea of blossom in the spring and heavy with fruit in the autumn. Fields thick with golden corn then shorn and left to stubble and dotted with stooks and the hop gardens curtained with golden clusters of catkin-like fruit then stripped and bare in August.

The hop pickers had long since folded their tents and returned to London's East End. The pungent smell of the drying hops no longer filled the air but the tall, conical, white-cowled oast houses still stood by the railway on which their crop would travel to

76

Borough Market in London.

Best had managed to find a compartment to himself and when not surveying the countryside as though seeing it through new eyes he took out the remaining unread letters from those responding to G.C.'s heart-rending newspaper advertisement. Most were similar to those he had already read, in that they wished her well, urged her to take heart, cursed her hard-hearted lover and enclosed 'a token to help you survive', 'a little financial assistance', 'an expression of sympathy to help you keep going', 'a mite'. But the penultimate letter was different. Written on pale-blue paper in an obviously feminine hand with many graceful loops and curlicues it spoke not of G.C.'s heartrending plea, nor urged her to take heart or enclose any money, it merely wanted to know what had happened to her brother, Edwin Bennett. 'I have been told how he was affected by your story, that it had weighed heavily upon him and he felt that he must do something to help you.' The writer went on to say that she had not heard from her brother for over two weeks.

This is very unusual, unheard of even. His manservant, who has not seen him for that time either, told me that he had been determined to seek you out. He felt that your situation had been preying on Edwin's mind, he being a very sensitive young man.

His friends are also at a loss to help me. I am at my wits' end trying to find him. Please tell me whether he did get in touch with you and, if so, when, and what came of the meeting. I am exhausting all the avenues and feel that should I not find my dear brother soon I shall begin to fear the worst and be obliged to seek help from the police.

This was all very curious. Several other gentlemen correspondents had expressed a desire to meet the poor abandoned girl. Did Mary and her older man friend encourage this in the hope of squeezing more money out of them? Or might this letter be an attempt at blackmail saying, in effect, 'I know what you are up to, and if you don't pay up...'? It ended on what could be taken as a threatening note or might merely read as a cry of sisterly despair.

If you can help me, please respond by return, otherwise I will be obliged to take the drastic step to which I referred. Yours sincerely, Violet Bennett

Again, Best itched to follow up this case.

During his early days at the Yard the rule was that if no complaint of fraud had been made or no prosecutor had come forward then no action would be taken. It was felt that if people were pursued merely on a detective's suspicion the liberty of the subject was put at risk. This policy gave great heart and encouragement to fraudsters and swindlers and they flourished.

Mr Vincent, however, had different ideas on the subject and when he became the director of the new CID the policy changed, and if they saw a suspicious advertisement in the newspapers they were encouraged to follow it up. Not now. Not with the Fenian threat demanding all their attention.

Best had fully expected his privacy to be disturbed at Chatham. This, after all, was England's largest naval base and dockyard as well as being the embarkation point for soldiers en route for India or whatever war was currently raging. But he was left to himself until just after the puffing and panting engine had reached the climax signalling imminent departure and the guard's whistle had been blown. Then the compartment door was flung open, two breathless men scrambled aboard and flung themselves on to the seats opposite Best. They looked harassed, anxious and sweaty as people do when they have made a desperate bid to catch a train. Despite the cold neither men wore overcoats or scarves.

Best waited for a moment or two for them to recover before nodding at them in a friendly fashion and murmuring, 'Good afternoon.'

The one sitting directly opposite Best managed a brief nod. He was a burly and sullen-looking fellow wearing a rough tweed jacket, a collarless shirt with frayed cuffs, knee breeches, a red and brown kerchief around his neck and a black cloth cap on his head.

His companion had not yet settled himself sufficiently to notice Best's welcoming gesture. He was hatless and conscious of it, continually running his hands over his grizzled close-cropped hair and straightening the edge of his collared waistcoat.

He kept shifting about in his seat and glancing anxiously out of the window. It was only after the train finally started and began to pick up speed that he took a deep breath, sat back in his seat and relaxed.

The next stop, the historic city of Rochester, was less than a mile from Chatham. Unlike that workaday town Rochester was gated, gabled, castled, cathedraled and altogether more dignified.

This was the heart of Charles Dickens country. Not only had the great author spent the happier part of his childhood here when his father worked in the Chatham docks but he had set some of the perambulations of the Pickwick Club in Rochester and Chatham and his fugitive convict Magwitch had prowled the dank Medway marshes nearby.

The Yard detectives felt they owed a great debt to Charles Dickens. They never forgot that it was he who, single-handedly, rescued them from the contempt in which they had been held ever since their birth in 1842 – a situation encouraged by a hostile and derisive press. Dickens had met and entertained the real life Scotland Yard detectives and lauded them in his magazine, *Household Words*. He found them to be an amiable brotherhood of respectable, keenly observant, perceptive, unusually intelligent men with 'good eyes' with which they looked you full in the face when they spoke. He had even based one of his fictional characters, the all-knowing Inspector Bucket of *Bleak House*, upon one of them, Inspector Charles Frederick Field, who had guided him around the stews of London's East End. He may have over-egged the pudding somewhat but his support had been much appreciated. He made them respected and admired and they never forgot that.

As they drew out of Rochester the sky darkened and the first snowflakes began to fall.

Eleven

The day had been a long and tiring one for Charlie Briggs, the guard on the London, Chatham and Dover express. It had begun in the chill early morning, three-quarters of an hour before the departure of the first Dover-bound boat train from Victoria Station.

First, he had made sure he had his whistle, carriage key, red and green flags, twelve detonators, a hand signal lamp and, not least, his book of Rules and Regulations. Then he checked that his watch and the guard's van clock agreed with the time shown on the station clock, which was adjusted twice daily to the exact mean time telegraphed from Greenwich.

After that, he had examined the company notices to see whether there was any matter regarding the Dover route requiring his particular attention, and seen that the carriages were correctly coupled and that the continuous brake in his van was in working order in case of emergencies.

As passengers began to arrive he kept an eye open to see that those getting into the first-class compartments were entitled to travel in them, that lone lady travellers were not put into smoking carriages and that, if possible, they were placed in ladies-only compartments. He ensured that only light articles were placed in overhead racks – heavier boxes and portmanteaux went under the seats or with him in his van. He checked any unaccompanied parcels against the weigh bills and signed for them and then, finally, began his journey record.

Charlie was noted both for his meticulous keeping of this detailed account and its neatness – much to the gratitude of the superintendent's clerk who had to sift through piles of such reports, many of which were not only barely legible but also spattered with blots and smudges of soot.

He took the same care over his appearance. His navy-blue uniform was always well-brushed and pressed, his cap peak shiny and his teeth and nails clean. He was an ex-sailor. Therefore, as well as disciplined personal habits, he brought to the job the skills of rope handling and knot tying – useful for securing piles of luggage.

Now his work day was ending at last. He had seen the passengers off, handed out their heavy luggage from his van, directed them towards omnibuses and cab ranks and wished them good evening. His guard's van was empty of luggage, none had gone missing and his journey record was complete.

There was only one more task to perform before he could go home to his wife Amelia and his young daughter, Alice, who would be waiting up so that he could read her a story from the *Infant's Magazine*, which he had found yesterday lying abandoned in a first-class carriage. Before the carriage washers went on board he must examine all the compartments to check that no personal property had been left behind nor damage done to LCDR property. Sometimes people were sick after a bad Channel crossing exacerbated by the rolling of the train and the smell of smoke from the engine. Then there might be burns to the upholstery, particularly serious when it occurred in a non-smoking compartment. Particulars of any damage would be added to his report, and while he would not exactly be blamed for burns on the upholstery in a non-smoking compartment, it would be felt that he might have noticed that someone was smoking in there. What chance he would have had to do that with all his numerous duties he did not know.

As it happened, not only did Charlie

Briggs's duties last well into the night but his report contained addenda of a much more serious nature than mere burns to LCDR armrests and cushions. He first peered into every open compartment then went back along, opening and examined those which still had their doors closed: three second class and one first class. He was relieved to see that the second class were all in good order and moved on to the one first-class compartment.

To his irritation he found the door handle was sticky, probably from the fingers of spoiled children allowed an excess of Dover rock or pink and white sugar mice. Such irritations usually occurred on the excursion trains, now that Dover was becoming such a family resort, not the Continental expresses. But, he reflected philosophically, sugary deposit was certainly preferable to the residue of sea-sickness.

He pulled out his handkerchief to wipe his hand but when he looked down at it he saw that his palm was dark red; the colour of drying blood.

Oh God! His worst dread. Someone had been attacked and robbed on his train.

This violence was becoming such a problem that passengers were demanding installation of the new electrical communication cords, which not only slowed the train down but also indicated the troubled compartment, instead of the rope-and-pulley type, which merely rang bells in the guard's van and the driver's cabin. Their alarm was only the old-fashioned type but he could swear he had not heard a bell ring and the driver hadn't mentioned hearing one either.

He breathed a sigh of relief when he opened the door and found the compartment empty. No crumpled body, minus watch and money, nor injured person slumped bloodily in the corner. Obviously the sticks of rock were coming in darker colours these days.

He looked all around the compartment but saw nothing troubling until he glanced at the floor. There, beside his left foot, was a black bowler hat.

Now that was unusual. Passengers didn't usually forget their hats. Gloves, yes, and spectacles and umbrellas. But you were undressed out of doors without a hat. You put it on automatically as you left the train, if you had ever taken if off.

Charlie knelt to retrieve it, leaning his right hand on the front of the seat cushion as he did so. As it sank in there was a squishing sound. A wetly squishing sound. He hesitated, knees still half bent, withdrew his hand from the upholstery and looked down at it.

This time his palm was not only wet and

red but also dotted with specks of white and across it lay two long dark hairs.

Charlie did not panic, or at least gave no outward appearance of doing so. He merely stood up, left the compartment, locked the door and made his way, rather rapidly, towards the station master, who was returning to his office after welcoming the boat train back to Victoria Station.

Best was one of the last passengers to leave the Continental express, having hung back so as not to bump into George R. Eventually he decided that enough time had elapsed. He gathered up his battered portmanteau and began to walk along the length of the empty train towards the ticket barrier.

Approaching him he saw a knot of men who had every appearance of being on an urgent errand. Slightly to the fore was a worried-looking guard. Close behind him was the top-hatted grave-faced station master and bringing up the rear was a railway policeman who looked as if he was desperately trying to recall 'appropriate action'. Best knew the feeling and recognized it.

The trio passed the LCDR's green, black and gold engine and one of the first-class carriages and came to a halt outside a compartment in the second. The guard was fumbling with his keys, attempting to fit one of them into the compartment door.

As Best drew alongside this worried trio the railway policeman recognized him and an expression of relief came over his face. Scotland Yard was close by and the detectives frequently had dealings with the LCDR police when making arrangements for extradition cases. As Briggs was turning the key the railway policeman drew the station master's attention by announcing, 'This is Detective Inspector Best of Scotland Yard.'

The station master looked up distractedly and gave him a curt nod.

'If I can be of any assistance,' offered Best. It was the last thing he wanted to be. He wanted to be home with Helen. But now could hardly just leave.

'We do not yet know with what we are dealing,' said the station master stiffly. Best shrugged, nodded and made as if to leave. The station master held out his hand and said in a more conciliatory manner, 'But we may yet be grateful for your advice, Inspector. The guard has found blood on the door handle and on the seat cushions.'

Charlie Briggs now had the door open. Best glanced inside and noted the lack of luggage and the hat lying on the floor. His heart sank. It was all too familiar and the lack of a body was no solace.

The first enquiry into a railway murder, committed by Franz Muller way back in 1864, had begun with an unnervingly similar scenario: blood on a door handle (but in that case on the inside) and soaked into a seat cushion. The dying victim had been found lying by the track some miles back on the North London line. They found the culprit, but had some difficulty in retrieving him from the United States, where he had fled, since Americans were angry that a British-built ship, the *Alabama*, had been running the North's blockade of the Southern ports.

Then, only two years ago, there had been almost a re-enactment of the Muller murder, this time on the London, Brighton and South Coast Railway, which operated from the terminal adjacent to the LCDR at Victoria. Again, the victim, already dead this time, was found beside the track and near a tunnel. Small wonder this trio looked so serious.

'So, who was in this compartment?' the station master asked Briggs after they had confirmed the presence of blood in the cushions.

'I'm not sure, sir.'

'You say that all the luggage has been claimed from your van?'

'Yes, sir.'

'And none was found in here?'

Best was not officially on the case yet but the railway police had made such a mess in their handling of the London, Brighton and SCR murder that the Yard would probably be called in quite soon, as they were then. But they would not thank him for bringing in another case at a time like this before it was absolutely necessary.

Best could feel the railway policeman looking at him. He knew why they were all hesitating. They didn't want to believe what their eyes and brains told them and were envisaging all the trouble and bad publicity this could bring to them and the company.

The railway policeman cleared his throat and offered hopefully, 'Maybe some drunks had a fight in here?'

The boat trains did sometimes have problems with passengers who drank heavily while on the ferries – out of fear or boredom. Best had not seen any drunks getting on this train but then he had only ventured out on a platform once to make a desperate dash to find a lavatory.

All heads turned to Charlie Briggs. It was one of the guard's jobs to look out for and if necessary eject drunken passengers and their luggage.

He shook his head. 'Weren't no drunken passengers on the train,' he said firmly.

Best could tell that the man was hoping

that this was the case. He sighed, then took a deep breath. If no one else was going to take charge here he'd better speak up – tactfully.

'Well, as you probably know, you will have to telegraph all stations, instructing them to search their nearby track, particularly in tunnels or just outside them. Also, you must stop every train and instruct the drivers to look out for a body – or bodies – lying beside the track.'

The station master, who had blanched at the mention of a body or bodies, now ceased being an ostrich and said to the railway policeman, 'Do as he says.' He turned to the guard. 'This carriage must be uncoupled immediately.'

'Yes, sir,' said Briggs. Clearly it was going to be some time before Alice heard her bedtime story.

Twelve

'O'Brien says that they are planning to bomb the railway stations and Scotland Yard,' said Best.

Robert Anderson, the Home Office adviser on Fenianism, nodded. 'I've heard that from my contacts.' Anderson, a vain little man, was in constant touch with a spy right at the heart of the Fenian organization in the United States but the Yard had no idea who the man was or how reliable his information. He, Vincent, Williamson, Littlechild and Best were back again in the Special Irish Branch office in the centre of Scotland Yard.

'What we need are details,' said Williamson as much to Anderson as to Best. 'Ernest, you'll have to keep in touch with O'Brien.'

Best nodded. 'Very well, but he's very frightened and might get suspicious if I probe any further at the moment. Particularly now he's home again.'

Williamson frowned. 'Suspicious? But does he realize you're a policeman?'

Best shook his head. 'No.'

Puzzled glances were exchanged.

'Well, *why* did he confide in you?' asked Anderson. 'What was his *purpose*?'

'He was sharing his worries with a friend. You know what it's like when you are away from home in a foreign country. Mere acquaintances become close confidants. You have a few drinks and tongues become loosened and your deepest secrets are revealed.'

Littlechild and Williamson nodded. They were policemen so they knew about the reactions of ordinary people. They had not been cushioned through life by 'connections' and background like Anderson and Vincent. They also knew about getting people to trust you while revealing nothing of yourself. Nothing important, anyway.

'So he doesn't know you've "passed it on" to the police?' asked Vincent wearily. It was no secret that the man had had enough of all this extra responsibility and wanted to leave now. Williamson was also weary of it but he did not have a wealthy wife to support him.

'Oh, yes. I told him that I knew someone in authority and would warn them to be vigilant.'

'We need names and dates,' said Vincent.

'He wouldn't give me any,' said Best, wondering why the man had to tell them what they already knew. 'As soon as I tried he became hesitant.' He glanced around at the curiously mixed group of men and wondered whether he could make them understand about O'Brien. 'He would never betray them,' he explained. 'He is very devoted to the cause – just doesn't like the idea of killing people to achieve its ends.'

Anderson slapped the table. 'Then we should arrest him and get it out of him.'

'With respect, that would achieve nothing,' said Best carefully. 'He hasn't confessed to any crime himself, merely knowledge of a possible one, and he could easily deny it, say he was drunk and let his imagination run away with him. Remind us that the Irish are good at telling stories, particularly to fox the English.'

'The only way to find out names and dates,' Williamson put in, 'is for those shadowing him to be more observant about where he goes and who he sees and for Inspector Best to extract more seemingly innocuous information from him out of which we may make some deductions.'

As they glumly pondered this Best stared out into the murky fog which hung low and lingered as usual among the Scotland Yard buildings. The dismal sight was made worse now that last night's snowfall was turning to dirty slush.

At least the melting snow should make searching the railway trackside easier. So far no body had been found, a fact greeted with great relief by the railway company, which preferred to believe that the blood-soaked upholstery was the result of a brawl and that the guard had failed in his duty by not noticing the drunken men as they boarded.

Best was not convinced, particularly since proper inspection had not been possible until daylight. He conceded that the heavy snow which had fallen during the night was unlikely to hide a body; such a mound would surely be obvious. But it might have covered something smaller such as a weapon.

'The whole world knows the Fenians are planning something serious soon,' Anderson insisted, indicating a copy of the *United Irishman*, which was full of dire threats, and another magazine which left little doubt about its aims: *Ireland's Liberator and Dynamite Monthly*.

'The Queen is becoming more and more nervous and the MPs are jumping at their own shadows and I'm not surprised!'

One of the regular suggestions in such Fenian magazines was that they should assassinate Queen Victoria. There had already been attempts on her life but these had been puny efforts by the deranged. A well-planned attempt involving dynamite was another matter. The Home Office was doing its best to guard the Queen by running 'pilot' locomotives in front of her train when she went to Balmoral and lining the track at vulnerable points with hundreds of railway plate-layers, although it had been pointed out that many of these railway workers would be Irish.

Assassination of heads of state seemed to be the answer to all national ills these days and dynamite was making it easier. US President Garfield had been shot three years ago but Tsar Alexander II had been killed with dynamite after several attempts plotted by Russian exiles in London. The British authorities tended to overlook this when they demanded that the United States should stamp out Irish threats to Great Britain. The British police *had* arrested Johan Most, the editor of a London-based German newspaper that had advocated the assassination of all heads of state and recommended dynamite for the purpose. He was found guilty of inciting murder and sent to prison for eighteen months.

'Right,' said Williamson. 'You keep up your lunchtime visits.'

'I won't be able to for much longer,' Best interrupted, causing raised eyebrows from Anderson and Vincent. 'Some old lag is bound to spot me.'

'True.' Littlechild nodded. 'Yard men are becoming too well known. Don't worry, I'll find you a new young detective who can come with you then take over.'

'But then he'd be connected with me,' Best pointed out, 'anyway a civilian might be better.' He hesitated then said, 'A woman, preferably.'

This proposition raised more eyebrows. There was nothing new in making use of the services of policemen's wives or sweethearts to accompany policemen when they were shadowing a suspect. A loving couple always looked less suspicious than a lone man and women had occasionally made enquiries by themselves, but only when a man was not suitable, such as when they wanted to trap an abortionist.

'I think it's the only way,' said Best.

'Very well,' said Williamson eventually.

Vincent nodded. 'But it will have to be someone very sensible.'

'Not Helen,' said Best quickly then stopped himself and explained, 'She'd be too easily connected with me – and,' he added lest they were thinking that it was all right to put someone else's wife at risk, 'she is too ... too...'

'Too ladylike and well spoken,' said Williamson rescuing him, 'so would be out of place on her own in a public house.'

97

'Right,' said Littlechild. 'I'll find you someone else.'

There had been a find beside the railway track. In fact two objects had been found. In this instance lying nowhere near a tunnel but in a lonely spot just outside the village of Newington, which lay between Sittingbourne and Chatham on the Dover to London route. This was cherry-orchard country, just south of the creek-ridden Medway estuary and its marsh villages.

The objects were spotted by Arthur Lewis, the young fireman on the 8.45 a.m. express from Victoria to the Medway port of Queenborough. Just before the train was due to branch off towards the Isle of Sheppey, on which Queenborough was situated, he had paused for a moment in his punishing task of shovelling sustenance into the ever-demanding mouth of the Europa Class 2–4–0 engine. As he did so, he glanced out of the cab to his left and spied something glinting among the fast-disappearing trackside slush and, beside that, a small mound of snow.

They passed the spot rapidly and he had been wiping the sweat out of his eyes at the time, so he had not been *quite* certain what he saw. Perhaps it was an old tin can that had caught the glow of the wintry early morning sun? On the return journey he looked again.

The snow had melted even more by then and the object became clearer. He was then certain that it was something quite sinister.

Lewis duly informed Mr Nathaniel Green, the station master at Chatham. He, truth to tell, was not too pleased to receive this information. He imagined that the matter of the bloody compartment had been resolved by the conclusion that it was the result of two drunks fighting.

He didn't want any more problems. He had enough with sailors running rampant after long periods at sea, not to mention bored and restless young soldiers awaiting embarkation for Egypt. Indeed, it was his opinion that if anyone had been fighting in the LCDR carriage it might well have been some of that soldiery. Nonetheless, Mr Green did his duty and sent out searchers. What they found gave the impression that Mr Green might be wrong or, at least, that the fight had been more murderous than he imagined.

Both objects were lying in Green's office when Best arrived, temporarily relieved of his duties at the Printers' Arms until O'Brien returned to England.

One was a knife; a double-edged knife made in England. The blade had been cleaned by the melting snow but traces of what appeared to be blood remained where the blade met handle. Of course, there was no way of telling whether this blood, if that was what it was, was animal or human.

The other, drying out near the office fire, was a felt hat. As it dried it began to regain its colour, changing from what had looked like black to a light grey. It was quite a splendid hat, the brim being wide and edged with a darker grey ribbon with a wide matching ribbon encircling the crown.

The sight gave Best a dreadful jolt. He clearly recalled seeing the hat for the first time being clamped to the head of George R. Hardinge to prevent the Dover winds from carrying it away. Had something terrible happened to that cheerful and gregarious Southern gentleman? He hoped not. But was not optimistic.

Of course, there was still no sign of a body and he knew that it was also possible that the hat was not a victim's but an assailant's. Hats, he had found, sometimes played a curious and unpredictable role in police enquiries. Indeed, Franz Muller, that first railway murderer, had been caught and executed largely due to hats – in the plural. When fleeing after his dreadful deed he had picked up the tall silk top hat of his victim, Thomas Briggs, and left behind his own rather stubby and oddly shaped hat. This was quickly identified. Foolishly, he kept

Briggs's silk topper but had altered it, probably because he had neither the time nor the money to buy a new one and would look conspicuous if he went bare-headed. At his trial Mr Briggs's hatter identified the top hat as one of his own make but explained that it had been 'cut down' – by someone who knew how to sew. Muller was a tailor. For a while Muller Cut-Downs became the latest fashion in gentleman's hats.

So, there was no certainty that George R. was the victim. After all, hadn't Best himself wondered whether the man was a Fenian sent to dispose of *him*?

Thirteen

Violet Bennett was a very calm young lady. Indeed, her demeanour struck Best as being rather at odds with the anxious pleas in her letter to G.C. which had begged for news of her brother, Edwin.

Since she lived in one of the grand stuccoed Bayswater terraces, Best had decided to visit her while on his way home to Notting Hill. He had gone on the spur of the moment, but by the time he was admitted to her presence in the large, airy drawing room he had become (uncharacteristically) a little concerned about how to present himself.

Not only was his visit unofficial but he was following up knowledge acquired in a possibly illegal manner – by persuading little Harry Rice to search his tenants' rubbish in pursuit of his whim. No crime had been reported nor injury claimed to justify his actions. Worse, by going to see Violet Bennett he might give hope where none existed of tracing her absent brother. Her possibly intentionally absent brother.

Violet Bennett had shown no feverish excitement nor anxious expectation at his arrival, as did some people when a Scotland Yard detective was announced. The slight, fair young lady had merely risen to greet him as though his visit was the most natural thing in the world.

Her air of tranquillity was almost palpable. But it was not, he soon realized, the bovine calm of the stupid or uncomprehending, nor the deliberately remote manner which some of the well-to-do adopted when meeting those whom they considered to be their social inferiors. The expression in her pale blue eyes was intelligent and warm as she listened to the detective inspector, who had decided that honesty would be the best policy. Well, almost.

While emphasizing that his visit was more or less unofficial he explained that her letter had been found, with others, 'among some rubbish which had been spilled onto the street and blown about a bit'. 'You would agree, I'm sure,' he went on, 'that the collection of rubbish is not what it used to be. It is in fact a disgrace to the capital.'

At the mention of her letter Violet gave a slightly perplexed frown but nodded for him to continue. The trick in such circumstances, Best knew, was to keep talking. Then, with luck, any gaps or inconsistencies in a story might fail to register. The human mind, he had found, was capable of taking in only so much information at a time and retaining even less.

'The person who found the letter,' he went on, 'an itinerant of my acquaintance, saw the word "police" in the text and, it being one of the few words which he recognized, he thought to bring it to me in the hope of gaining a reward.' Rice, he knew, would certainly not want to broadcast his scrabbling among the detritus of the life of his tenants.

'As for your brother's absence, you probably know that an adult person may absent themselves at their will, and as long as there are no suspicions of foul play the police are not obliged to try to trace them.'

She nodded again, her eyes remaining calmly fixed on his face while her body remained perfectly still. It might appear that she had no real anxiety about her brother's disappearance but Best had noticed that she had received him after only a short delay and before changing from her walking dress and fur-trimmed walking boots. Obviously, he had caught her just as she returned home, possibly after a stroll in nearby Hyde Park.

'However,' he went on, 'I was struck by the genuine tone of your plea and, it just so happened, that I had noticed G.C.'s advertisement in a newspaper.' That part, at least, was absolutely true.

Why am I talking and even thinking in this precise manner, he wondered, like a character in a Jane Austen novel? Maybe it was that Miss Bennett's solemn but calm demeanour seemed to demand a thoughtful and precise explanation.

So, therefore, he explained, given her letter and the advertisement, he had decided to come to speak to her on his way home. But she must understand that he was acting entirely of his own volition and his visit should not, at this juncture at least, be looked upon as official. If she thought his interference was impertinent and wished him to leave she only had to say so.

At this she held up her hand and said in a

soft, low voice, 'Oh, no, please. I am very grateful for your interest. I have been grappling alone with this matter.' She held out her hands again and explained in a matter-of-fact tone, which made it clear that she was not seeking sympathy, 'My parents are both dead, and I have been at a loss as to what to do.' She tilted her neat little fair head just a fraction to one side and gave him a fleeting half-smile. 'Therefore I should be grateful for any advice and assistance you could offer me.'

Even while voicing this concern and making this plea there remained a remarkable serenity about her. There was a quietness, too, in her dress which was elegant but not the height of fashion.

The draped apron overskirt of her pale golden gown was gathered back in a restrained *à la Polonaise* style rather than a small bustle, which – to Helen's disgust – was making its return. His wife was of the opinion that when women indulged in such extreme, unnatural exaggerations of the female form they encouraged men not to take them seriously.

'First, tell me about your brother. How he conducts his life, his habits and so forth.'

She leaned forward slightly and began to explain that Edwin was her sole close relative and that he was a wealthy young man who, being the only son, had inherited the family fortune. However, she spread her hands and looked about her, he had been most generous with her and their aunt with whom she lived.

It transpired that Edwin Bennett was thirty-five years of age, unmarried and living in a grand villa just down the road by leafy Holland Park. He did not go out into society very much, preferring to spend his time doing good works through the Church and on his own initiative, although he was fond of the opera and the more serious theatre, to which she often accompanied him. He was not at all profligate but wanted to spend most of his money helping others less fortunate.

Violet and Edwin were in frequent touch. He often called on her on his way up to town or to his church, which was nearby.

'But I have not seen him now for almost three weeks, and that is most unusual.' As she said this her hand crept to the lace frill around the neck of her dress and stayed there, fingering it. This, for her, he realized, was a sign of agitation or concern.

Edwin's servants had told her that he had gone out one afternoon, and never returned. At first they had not been concerned. Mr Bennett was wont to get 'caught up in things and want to follow them through' and, in any case, it was not their place to point out his absence to his sister. He might not want her to know where he was.

Best thought that a little curious. He also thought it a little strange that the man should have chosen not to live with his only sister, who seemed a very amiable if constrained young woman, but had set up a separate establishment close by. That was being profligate, surely? But then, maybe it was understandable that a young man would want his privacy. But to do what? Good works?

Of course it could be that Edwin Bennett *was* profligate in another sense of the word. Maybe the saintly young man was a rake or had more unusual tastes? Then again, maybe the aunt was a dragon or a silly old woman whom Edwin couldn't stand?

In any event, neither his servants nor his friends were able to suggest where he might have gone. Enquiries had also been made among those who benefited from his largesse, to no avail. But, eventually, his manservant had recalled that just before he had gone missing he had been very touched by G.C.'s advertisement in the newspaper and had expressed his intention to seek out the unfortunate young lady.

Best took a deep breath, assured Violet Bennett that he understood her concern, reiterated a person's right to go where they would but admitted that the circumstances were a little unusual.

'You will appreciate,' he told her, 'that we at Scotland Yard are very taken up at present with preventing another Fenian outrage. But I will, on my own initiative, make discreet enquiries to clarify the matter – as and when my other duties allow.'

'I'd be very grateful.' A tear started into her eye. 'I am *very* concerned.'

He obtained her assurance that she would notify him the instant that Edwin reappeared, and took Edwin's address and those of his friends.

Perhaps servants and friends would disclose something to him that they were loath to divulge to Violet, his calm little sister.

The following day was his first back at the Printers' Arms and, en route, he revisited the excitable little Harry Rice.

'I've got a lot more for you,' he exclaimed, fishing a crumpled sheaf of letters from a drawer under his filthy kitchen table. 'Hard work collecting these, sifting through all that much, I can tell you.'

Ah, he was becoming braver and a touch resentful. Thought he should be dropped something for his trouble.

'Worth it, though,' said Best coldly, 'saving

you from prosecution for offences against the Act.' He glanced around meaningfully.

Rice was easily intimidated and after a short silence nodded, 'Oh, yes. Yes.'

'What I want to know about,' said Best in a friendlier tone, 'is gentlemen callers. Do they have many?'

'Oh, I wouldn't know about that. Not my business. Not my business.' The knowing look in his eyes conveyed he knew a lot and would tell if...

Best sighed. 'Mr Rice, I'll repeat, do they get many gentlemen callers?'

Rice thought for a moment then, obviously realizing that there were to be no rich pickings in this, but could be trouble, said, 'Oh, yes. Now and then.'

'Right.' Best waited.

' 'E always goes out when they come.'

This was more like it.

'What are they like? Are they poor men?'

Rice smirked. 'Shouldn't think so!' He was back in his element, gossip and prurient interest in his lodgers. He began to grow excited. 'Flush, I'd say they were. Some of them 'ave the key to the bank all right.' His eyes lit up and began swivelling about.

'Do they get many of these gentlemen callers?'

'No,' he admitted. 'Like I says, just now and then.'

'Always on their own.'

He nodded. 'Oh, yes.'

Best wondered how 'Mary' justified the easy circumstances in which she lived, if these were, as he suspected, young men following up the G.C. advertisement. Why, in fact, she did not elect to meet them away from her lodgings. Wouldn't that make it easier for her to pretend poverty and desperation and also be more suitable behaviour for a respectable lone woman?

Harry Rice grinned suddenly. 'You think they're trying to take 'em for more than those letters bring in?'

Best looked at him. He hadn't thought about it but of course the man had read the letters to find out what all the fuss was about. Natural curiosity. He'd have done the same himself. He realized he would soon have to start paying him to keep his mouth shut.

'I don't know *what* I think just yet,' he answered truthfully. 'But,' he fixed Rice with a cold eye, 'I *am* trusting you to keep this business to yourself.' He glanced about him meaningfully.

'Oh, course. Course, Mr Best.' He paused then grinned again. 'Clever, though, ain't it? Very clever.'

'Don't worry, they won't prosper,' Best warned but he was not sure of that. He took

110

out a photograph of Edwin Bennett given to him by Edwin's calm sister. 'Is this one of the men who called?'

Rice contemplated the head-and-shoulders photograph of the charitable Edwin in which his full-whiskered face gazed thoughtfully out into the far distance to his right. Rice took the portrait over to the window, which admitted a little more dismal light into the wretched basement room. He was making a meal of this.

'Well?'

Eventually, he shook his head. 'Can't say in all honesty that 'is face is familiar to me.'

Fourteen

Arthur Sidgewick was a curious sort of fellow, Best decided. The man's instant reaction when Best presented himself at the door of Elgin House was surprise and suspicion. Surely he had realized that if she had not gone to the police, Miss Bennett might hire a private detective to find her brother? However, once this gentleman's gentleman was certain that Best's credentials were bona fide he had gradually become more compliant, although the detective still got the feeling he did not welcome the intrusion.

'You must understand my position,' he warned Best. 'If I carelessly reveal my master's personal matters he will no longer trust me, and,' he spread his hands meaningfully, 'without trust I am unemployable.'

Best was not sure he would trust him anyway. He found it more than a little strange that the man had waited for almost two weeks before alerting Miss Bennett of her brother's disappearance. It might be, of course, that he disliked having his fiefdom invaded by women. In Best's experience bachelors' servants usually had much more power and freedom than those in houses where there was a woman to keep an eye on things.

Not that there was any air of neglect about this residence. Naturally there was an absence of the fripperies and draperies produced by ladies with empty hours to fill: painted, appliquéd, beaded or embroidered fire-screens, mantel valances and antimacassars sometimes so heavily stitched as to make it almost impossible to rest your head on them. Despite the absence of the owner the villa gave every appearance of being the well-kept home of a bachelor of some considerable wealth. The furniture committed neither the sin of being all new and soulless or all depressingly fussy and old fashioned but was a pleasant blend of the two. The lighting, however, was electric.

Best was inclined to agree with the Professor of Chemical and Forensic Medicine who had written to *The Times* a few years ago asserting that electricity could never be used as a room illuminant because it was too strong and, unlike gas, not adjustable. To back his argument he had described how, after being subjected to electric light for three hours, its blue rays had haunted him and he had suffered from an intense headache.

Well, here it was lighting the room. Its glaring effect was somewhat softened by stained-glass shades but it was still brighter than anything Best had experienced indoors and he found it quite disturbing. He was thankful that he at least was not going to be subjected to its rays for three hours!

It was quite understandable that a wealthy young bachelor would want to sample the latest appliances but the man described by his sister had not seemed to be the sort who would feel it necessary to be ahead of the fashion in this manner. Maybe she didn't know him as well as she thought she did?

Sidgewick seemed perfectly at ease under

the electricity's bright glow. Was that what disturbed Best about this tall, well-set-up man with a perhaps too-confident manner? That he seemed too much at ease, as though *he* were the master here? He described himself as personal servant, valet and steward and informed Best that there was also a butler in situ. Ah, now, there was a recipe for dissent. Butlers were a fearsome breed who vied with the wives for control of a home and would probably do the same with such an influential manservant.

Sidgewick could offer very little information about Edwin Bennett's friends and social contacts that had not already been gleaned from the sister. It had occurred to Best that financial problems might account for the young master's absence but rather than enquire directly he decided to approach the matter obliquely by appealing to Sidgewick's vanity. He slid his notebook into his jacket pocket and made as if to leave. Then he hesitated and enquired casually, 'Does Mr Bennett confide in you with regard to his financial matters, by any chance?'

Sidgewick smiled in a slightly superior manner. 'Oh yes. Of course.' He smiled again, the scar, which pulled at his upper lip, managing to convert the expression into something slightly sinister. 'Mr Bennett has little patience with such matters himself,' he said, then added hurriedly, 'as I'm sure he would be the first to admit.'

He's covering himself in case the man returns, thought Best. At least that indicated that he was not certain whether he had gone for good.

'And his affairs – they are in order?'

'Oh, yes.' Sidgewick was about to continue but stopped abruptly.

'I ask you, of course,' said Best a little icily, 'only as a means to help establish possible reasons for his departure. As you know, financial matters can...'

'Oh, of course. Of course,' said Sidgewick in a more conciliatory manner. 'I understand. No. There is no problem.' He took a deep breath and explained, 'Most of Mr Bennett's stocks and shares are in railways, coal and cotton. Now, as you may be aware, the cotton trade was dealt a severe blow by the American Civil War but matters improved when it ended, by which time other sources of raw cotton had been developed. Now, of course, we do have the problem of this increasing foreign protectionism with regard to our manufactured goods and our foolish exportation of machinery is not helping. We're giving foreigners the means to produce their own!' He threw his hands in the air. 'Are we mad?'

He was certainly knowledgeable but in

reality had told Best only as much as could be gleaned from the financial pages of any newspaper. But Best knew how to play this game. He purported to be impressed and commented, 'You are well informed, I must say.' He paused and nodded. 'So, like everyone else, Mr Bennett has been somewhat affected by all this?'

Sidgewick shrugged and compressed his lips. 'Somewhat. But to no great consequence. He has hardly had to touch his capital.'

Hardly.

'But he *has* spent some of it of late?'

'Only a little, a very little.'

'Recently?'

Once you actually got people talking on forbidden subjects and kept the conversation going it tended to gather its own momentum, almost as though permission to speak had been given. There was also the fact that servants couldn't resist being taken seriously for once, which was why Best always spent so much time buttering them up.

'Well, strangely enough,' admitted the manservant, 'on the very day he disappeared he instructed me to dispose of quite a large amount of railway scrip.'

'And you did so?'

'The day after.'

Best nodded and said casually, 'Well, that

could be important.'

That could be *very* important. Has he told me that in case I find out about it and draw some damaging conclusions? Or am I really becoming too suspicious about people?

Helen, when he told her, thought perhaps he was. 'Honestly, Ernest, just because there was a spate of servants who murdered their employers, now you have to suspect them all!'

'No, I don't. It's just that they are so conveniently placed to get up to mischief, aren't they? Look how many are charged with stealing from their employers.'

'Yes, and aren't the servants always the first to be accused? Sometimes unjustly.'

'And often justly.' He sighed. 'The sad truth is we have to look first at those who have the opportunity.'

'So,' she said not acquiescing but changing the subject, 'how are you going to occupy yourself now that you don't have to spend every lunchtime at the Printers' Arms?'

'Well,' he said, 'I've been given a group of Fenian-watchers to organize, and,' he added ruefully, 'if I have any time left I'll be allowed to catch up with my other cases.'

'Finding Mr Bennett?'

'Ah, well, he is still unofficial. So I won't have much time to go chasing after him.'

'Poor Miss Bennett will be left worrying,

then?'

'Maybe not.'

He concentrated on soaking the last smidgeon of steak and kidney pudding in the gravy.

'What do you mean? You're being inscrutable, Ernest, it doesn't suit you.'

He grinned. 'I mean I may be writing a letter to G.C. myself.'

Helen frowned suspiciously. 'What's the point of that?'

'To suggest that we meet and hint that I have the means to assist her.'

Helen looked startled. 'You won't go, will you?'

He nodded. 'Of course. If I'm invited.'

She contemplated this answer silently for a moment before saying very seriously, 'But that might be dangerous, Ernest.'

'I won't take unnecessary risks.'

'But a man who did that is missing!'

'We don't *know* that he wrote to her. Only that Sidgewick said he wanted to help her.'

'But it's a *possibility*.' Her voice was rising. It sometimes struck Best as rather droll that although it had proved so difficult to win this lady whose main fear had been that marriage would prevent her continuing her career as an artist, now that they were married she was desperately afraid she would lose him.

He patted her hand and gave her a reassuring smile. 'There's one big difference between me and Edwin Bennett.'

'What's that?' she snapped.

'I am forewarned.'

Fifteen

Hannah Barker was late for work. The housekeeper would not like that. 'I *knew* I shouldn't have taken on a person who lived out,' Mrs Harris would say. 'I *knew* this would happen.'

In fact it didn't happen that often. Hannah was desperate to keep her job as a scullery maid at Locksley Hall, even though it meant leaving home some mornings before the sun rose.

She would always make sure she was well on her way by five thirty. But she had been kept awake all night by the baby's teething cries. She had finally fallen asleep at four o'clock so that when the alarm howled for attention at quarter to five her automatic re-action was to shut off the dreadful noise immediately so she might sink back into blessed oblivion.

Fortunately, the alarm had re-awoken the baby. She began to whimper, then cry a little, then screech loudly. Eventually, the penetrating sound acted as a second alarm and rocketed Hannah out of her bed in a panic.

There was nothing for it, after leaving the baby with her mother, but to take the short cut through the fields and across the railway line. She hadn't been that way for some time, partly because her shoes were so thin. They would become soaked by the early morning dew and then she would have to spend the day with sodden feet while trying to hide the fact from Mrs Harris.

There *were* other reasons why she should not take that route. The farmer on the near side of the track became enraged when people used his land as a shortcut and crossing the railway line like that was not only dangerous but against the law. Last, but certainly not the least consideration, was that Lord Beckton, the master at the hall, not only expected his servants to be respectable and stay out of trouble but he did not like them gaining access to his estate through gaps in its hedges and fences. He claimed it encouraged poachers to do the same. Hannah knew that was nonsense. The poachers got in anyway, making their own gaps where necessary.

But today Hannah was so late that she had no time to go to the railway footbridge further down the track. She must take the short cut, so she left Holly Lane through the gate that opened into Friar's Field.

The night had been bitterly cold, resulting in a thick hoar frost. It clung to the hedges and skeletal trees, coated the yellowing grasses on the field's edges causing them to stand up with an unnatural stiffness, and lay almost like a snowdrift across the centre. In fact, the whole scene was quite magical, bathed as it was in the golden glow of dawn. Like an illustration from a fairy tale; the Snow Queen perhaps.

But Hannah was too agitated to appreciate this beauty. If she hurried she might just reach the hall in time to keep her job.

Her footsteps crackled as her feet crushed and snapped the icy stalks and fractured small patches of ice. It occurred to her how unfair it was that she should be making her way over this freezing field in her thin dress, feet already soaked and bitterly cold, while her mistress lay in a warm canopied bed and would remain there for at least another five hours.

But this resentful thought was driven from her mind in an instant by the sight that greeted her as she reached the fence which guarded the London, Chatham and Dover Railway line.

Best breezed into the Printers' Arms, turning his head to his left as he entered ready to greet his old friend O'Brien who was in his usual spot in the corner by the fire.

Seeing him there he began to smile in easy recognition. Then he noticed that the Irishman was not alone and that the glance he threw Best was guarded to say the least. He did smile and nod, 'Hello, Ernest,' but it was the smile and nod of an acquaintance, a fellow pub habitué.

Best quickly toned down his expression to that of a casual grin and gave a slight inclination of his head. He avoided looking back at O'Brien's companion but the glimpse he had had of him had been enough.

The face was squarish, the hair ginger and the expression amiable but the eyes were gimlet and alert. Their glance had swept over him from head to toe.

It was the glance, almost, of a detective. A clerk at Scotland Yard had once told Best that he could always spot a plain-clothes detective the minute he entered a room. 'Their eyes rake around in one sweep. Then they settle – with their backs to the wall, so they can see what's going on and no one can sneak up behind them.'

Best did none of these things. He ambled towards the bar, keeping his head still and his glance directly ahead. As he went, he greeted other acquaintances with more friendliness than he had shown O'Brien.

He stood by the bar chatting to them and the landlord, ordered his usual pint and, on this occasion, food; the ordinary, which today was roast beef. Meanwhile, he tried to decide whether to go over and join O'Brien and his new friend. To do so might invite further scrutiny and suspicion from the stranger. Not to do so might invite even more suspicion.

The question was settled by O'Brien, who waved and beckoned him over calling out, 'Come and join us, Ernest.'

Best held up his right hand in casual acknowledgement. 'Be right there.' But he deliberately kept talking for a while longer before going over.

He had to tread carefully until he was sure how much this stranger knew about him and O'Brien before he became drawn into conversation. Did he know about Paris, for instance?

Again, O'Brien paved the way. After introducing his friend, Joseph Flinn, he said, 'I was just telling Joe how we bumped into each other in Paris like that!'

Best shook his head in wonderment.

123

'Amazing. It was amazing. I couldn't believe it!' He laughed. 'It was the only cheerful thing that happened to me while I was there!' He shook his head again and raised his glass to both of them. 'The French are trying to put a brave face on it – saying they are past the worst and all that but...' he grimaced. 'I don't know, I don't know. Doesn't look like it to me.'

Joe looked puzzled.

'Ernest writes about wine,' explained O'Brien.

'Oh, sorry!' laughed Best. 'I'm so obsessed by it all and the terrible situation over there that I forget that not everyone is!'

'It would be this disease of the vine you're talking about, would it?' enquired Flinn.

'Yes, yes.' Best took a sup of his ale and put his glass down before saying, 'Bad business. Bad business.'

'I thought it was getting better now?'

Best waved his right forefinger knowingly. 'That's what they would like you to believe, but...'

He described his meetings with the experts and the government spokesman and explained the situation in detail – sufficiently, he hoped, to show that there was nothing on his mind but wine production and its problems and thus no room in it for anything like Fenians, crime, informers or fiendish devices.

He was gratified to see Flinn's eyes glaze over and realized he had succeeded in making himself look like a harmless and garrulous fool obsessed with the evil aphid, phylloxera. Better not make too good a job of it or Flinn might wonder why O'Brien had sought out his company. Best had learned the art of boring by studying George, a court gaoler whose colleagues found him so tedious that they made sure he was always given charge of the prisoners. They had no one to talk to while waiting in their cells so even George's endless monotone was music to their ears.

Flinn looked relieved when Best's food arrived and he settled down to enjoy it. O'Brien was also looking relieved, if a little puzzled, but Best imagined that this was for a different reason. Despite his splendid performance he noticed that Flinn still watched him closely. Almost as if he were photographing him with his eyes and filing the negative for future reference.

Between bites Best endeavoured to be a little more entertaining. He was relieved to see that the new barmaid was in place. She was the wife of an East End constable. He could make his exit now and decided to make it swiftly.

He used the last roast potato to soak up the remaining gravy and spiked the final piece of beef to go with it and sighed. 'I'm going to miss this.' He popped the forkful into his mouth and chewed appreciatively.

'Off on your travels again, Ernest?' asked O'Brien, surprised.

Best shook his head and pushed his plate away. 'No. Giving it up. For the moment, anyway. I've got a commission to write a book on wine and the ravages of phylloxera so I'm taking some time off to do it.'

'Oh, well, we'll miss you,' said O'Brien. He feigned regret but Best could sense that the man was extremely relieved. This should show any observers, like Flinn, that they were not meeting so he could pass on information to Best and would therefore lessen the likelihood of a scene such as the one which had occurred recently in O'Ryan's Liquor Saloon in New York.

A journalist, Red Jim McDermott, had been enjoying a boozy lunch with a leading Skirmisher, O'Donovan Rossa, when two men strode into the bar. One of them pulled out a bulldog revolver and took direct aim at the journalist. Despite being at such close quarters the shot missed and the man fled but left a card announcing that Red Jim was in the pay of the British government and that he had died at the hands of an Irish avenger who had travelled three thousand miles (from Cork) to get him. There were wry comments from Fenians who claimed that he really *would* have died had the attempt been made by an Irish-American with Civil War experience. The two would-be assassins were caught but since no one in the bar had seen a thing the case against them was dismissed.

It sometimes seemed to Best that the Fenians spent most of their energies trying to kill each other, but he could understand their difficulties.

'Well, it's been nice knowing you,' said O'Brien as he stood up to shake Best's hand when he left. 'Maybe we'll meet again sometime.'

Flinn nodded his goodbye. 'Pleased to meet you.' He spoke amiably but his eyes were cold.

Best nodded and laughed. 'Sorry to go on and on about the little yellow aphid!'

Flinn smiled faintly. 'Oh, don't we all feel strongly about something or other.'

The body lay a few paces to the east of the gap in the fence where you could get onto the railway track just by tipping one of the posts to one side.

The man lay face downwards, right hand outstretched as though grasping for something that was not there, the cape of his Inverness overcoat thrown up over his head.

Like everything else in the field that morning the body was dusted with sparkling frost, but there were darker patches where the sun had begun to melt the white layer. Obviously, the overcoat had been soaked by the previously melting snow and the icy overnight temperatures had refrozen the wet material.

When she first saw the body Hannah let out a terrible scream and ran away. But she came back. Now she stared down at it for several moments, her mouth opening and closing as if about to scream again, but realized no one would hear her except maybe the person who had done this. She looked about her fearfully. An eerie silence was closing in on her. She could not move. In a strange way everything seemed so normal – apart from this body lying there cold and still.

She turned. She must get away and tell someone! She was about to climb through the fence, run over the track and dash up to the hall when she realized how bad things looked for her. She should not be here. She had been warned not to come this way. She would probably lose her job this time. What would she do for money if she were sacked? Her mother had none and their local poorhouse was a desperate place.

She racked her brains for an excuse for

being there but came up with none. She *could* just go on and not tell anyone what she had found. It was a terrible temptation but she knew it would be a great sin.

I know, she thought suddenly. I could say that a little boy had told me that there was something strange down by the railway track in Friar's Field! But they would ask her which little boy and she couldn't say she didn't know. Everyone knew everybody around here and in any case she'd never been any good at telling lies. She stood there staring and shivering. When she finally realized that she could not leave the poor man there and not tell anybody, she began to cry.

Then she wiped her face on her shawl and told herself not to be such a coward and that maybe the poorhouse was not as bad as they said. She stumbled forward, pushed her way through the fence, crossed the line, scrambled through the other fence and began to run towards the hall, sobbing and shivering as she went.

Sixteen

Constable Rawston of the Kent County Constabulary contemplated the body with some alarm. He had quickly realized this was not one of the usual sudden deaths caused by a heart attack or a farm injury or as the result of a drunken brawl. To begin with the man was obviously not from these parts; neither an agricultural worker nor a landowner. His clothes were not only fashionable and expensive but out of the ordinary. Foreign-looking, in fact. Was he French? The only Frenchmen they saw around here were onion sellers. And what a strange place for such a man to be lying – on the edge of a Kentish field beside a railway track in the middle of nowhere!

The strangest part was yet to come.

When the body was turned over to be placed on a door by two farm labourers, PC Rawston realized that this must in fact be a murder and, again, a most unusual one for this neighbourhood. Drunken brawls produced black eyes and faces puffy from punches, and perhaps a wound from a knife or club. It was hard to tell from the fast-decomposing face whether it had been punched but, to judge by the blood-soaked shirt, this was not the result of one angry drunken blow but more of a frenzied attack. He must send a message to the divisional superintendent as soon as possible so they could send out one of those headquarters detectives.

These decisions made, he was about to tell the men to carry the body away to the make-shift mortuary in the King of Mercia public house when he heard a shout. He looked up to see Lord Beckton, followed by a retinue of servants, riding across the field towards them. His groom and his scullery maid, Hannah Barker, were keeping up as well as they could and tripping over the still-frozen stubble as they went.

Lord Beckton was not only the most important landowner around here but chairman of the bench and of their police watch committee, so when he called out for them to stop, it was sensible to do so. He was a decent enough employer by all accounts, so long as you doffed your cap and bowed low enough.

'It was my servant Hannah here, who found the body!' exclaimed Lord Beckton as he arrived. He looked behind him for the confused and breathless young woman coming up in his wake. 'The girl acted very responsibly. She did not panic or throw a fit but very bravely ran to us to sound the alarm. We, of course, sent for you.'

Rawson nodded and touched his shako cap lightly. 'Thank you sir.'

He could guess what Hannah was doing down here at that time of day but if Lord Beckton wasn't going to object to her climbing through his fence why should he?

What wasn't so clear was why the landowner himself had come. 'I've brought her here so you can question her and, of course, to offer you any assistance you may need.'

Rawston realized that this 'gentleman' was probably no different from other people: he wanted to know what was going on and to be in on all the excitement, then he could tell the tale to all his friends later and be even more puffed up with importance than usual. But Rawston said, 'Thank you, sir. Be helpful if you could have someone ride over to inform the superintendent.'

Beckton nodded his assent, dismounted, handed the reins over to his groom and looked over the body and muttered, 'Hmph. Obviously a gentleman. Poor fellow, poor fellow.' His glance fastened on the now-bloody waistcoat and the shoes. 'And an

American gentleman if I'm not mistaken.'

How did he know that? The servants and labourers exchanged surprised glances and began whispering to each other. Lord Beckton silenced them with a glance but Jake Butfoy, one of the labourers, whose chest was twice as wide and deep as Lord Beckton's, kept clearing his throat noisily. Finally, he raised his hand and said, 'Scuse me. Scuse me.'

Lord Beckton was about to silence him as well when Rawston asked, 'What is it, Jake?'

Jake looked about him bashfully, disconcerted to find himself the centre of attention, but managed to stutter throatily, 'They've ... they've been searching the track.'

'Who has?'

'The railwaymen.'

Everyone knew that Jake's brother, Albert, manned a signal box at a level crossing down the line.

'What for?'

'They didn't want it to get out. Bad for the company.' They could see he wished he hadn't spoken now. Didn't want to be responsible for throwing his brother out of work.

'What get out, Jake?' persisted Rawston patiently, lifting his chinstrap and pushing his hat to the back of his head in a subconscious effort to appear less official and intimidating.

Albert opened his mouth, then closed it again while they all waited tensely.

'Don't worry about Albert,' said Lord Beckton suddenly. 'I'll see he's all right.'

Jake took heart at that, cleared his throat again and this time launched forth with his tale and didn't stop.

'When the Dover Express got back to Victoria they found a compartment all covered in blood. It looked bad and they thought it might be another robbery like they had on the Brighton line so they searched by the track to see if they could find a body but there weren't none. So they decided it must have been a drunken brawl. Some sailors or something – even though it were in first class.'

'And they didn't inform us!' exclaimed Lord Beckton.

'Well, I reckon they thought it could have happened anywhere on the line. They didn't know where, and,' repeated Jake, 'they wanted to keep it quiet, like.'

Everyone looked at the gap in the fence. He must have come the other way – from the trackside. Maybe escaping from someone or hoping to find help? But he had been too badly injured to stagger more than a couple of feet. The thought was a sobering one, particularly as the man was a guest in their country.

'That's very helpful, Jake,' said Rawston. 'It helps solve the mystery of how the man got here and shows us what to do next.'

Jake blushed self-consciously. His moment in the limelight was over but it was clear from the glances of his neighbours that his status had been raised. He'd be listened to in the King of Mercia tonight.

Rawston's reaction was a mixture of relief and disappointment. This might turn out to be a railway police case. But, then, perhaps not. After all, the body had been found within their jurisdiction.

In fact it turned out to be a three-force case: Kent County, the LCD Railway and the Metropolitan Police in the form of the already involved Detective Inspector Ernest Best. Largely Best's, however. The railway did not have a force adequate enough to cope and Kent County were only too happy to hand over the responsibility. That way they would save themselves the expense and manpower. Also, they would avoid all the criticism which would be heaped upon the police when, as doubtless would occur with such a difficult case, it remained unsolved.

Seventeen

She was a skinny little thing, no more than sixteen or seventeen years old and very nervous, keeping her eyes down and balling her small hands into tight fists.

Best wasn't surprised. She was the first to be heard. The first to be obliged to sit alone in a wide open space in front of all those people, some of them very important locally. They stretched around her in a semi-circle, all eyes upon her. The coroner, Dr Washman, had given her special dispensation to sit, seeing as she was so young, and nervous and with child again.

He kept encouraging her to speak up, gently leading her into her testimony and, eventually, she managed to take up her tale about finding the body at dawn and running to tell them at Locksley Hall. She never mentioned why she was at that particular spot at that hour of the morning and he didn't ask.

Rawston had put Best in the picture and

commented that doubtless Lord Beckton had had a word with the coroner and asked him to refrain from mentioning the subject. He'd pointed out his Lordship, a tall, spare man sitting to the right of the coroner – not to any particular purpose as far as Best could see. He wasn't part of the jury who sat in a row to the left, just one of these grandees who thought it their right to sit alongside the coroners and magistrates even if they weren't on the bench themselves.

Apparently, around here, Lord Beckton's requests were commands but Best doubted whether the newspaper reporters sitting at the back of this upstairs room at the King of Mercia would be so circumspect about the offence of trespassing committed by an employee of a railway shareholder and board member. But doubtless the newspaper owners were also friends of Lord Beckton as fellow board members so it would all end up the same anyway.

Readers of the *Kentish Independent* might guess what his scullery maid was doing down by the railway track at dawn but the metropolitan readers of *The Times* and *Daily Telegraph*, if they thought of it at all, would imagine that was just one of the strange things that poor country folk did. Stealing coal that fell from the engines, perhaps?

Everyone knew that the real excitement of

the case centred around the fact that this was another railway murder. Already, as before, there were demands for more security for passengers. Goodness knows they paid enough for the fares, particularly on these Continental expresses. Instead of separate compartments where they were locked in cheek by jowl with who knows what villain, why could they not have long open carriages with seats either side of a central walkway as they did in the United States of America? Not private enough for us British, others responded. The Americans might not mind being herded together like cattle, the English would.

What about better lighting? They were experimenting with electricity on the London to Brighton Pullmans but why not in all carriages? Much too bright and glaring to be tolerated in such an enclosed space, retorted the opposition. The only people to benefit would be the chemists who sold the aspirin to alleviate the resulting headaches.

But of course what was attracting the most attention was the mystery of it all and the fact that the victim appeared to be a wealthy American.

Appeared to be because, as yet, he had to be properly identified, which was one of the reasons why Best was attending the inquest. But although he had been able to confirm that this was definitely his fellow passenger on the *Calais–Douvres*, who had introduced himself as George R. Hardinge from Georgia, he admitted that at present there was no way of being certain that he was who he had said he was. Telegraph messages had been sent to the police in Georgia, however, and they were making enquiries.

PC Rawston, the second witness to give evidence, had even commented jokingly, 'He could have been murdered in mistake for you! You look a bit like him, you know.'

That gave Best a jolt. He understood what the village constable meant. They were both rather 'colourful' in their dress, particularly in the eyes of a rural population for whom, Best knew, 'standing out' was something that would be avoided at all costs. He also knew that a police 'spy' was a much more likely target than an American on a mission to help the French with their wine problems. But Rawston was unaware of the Fenian connection so there was no sound reason for his comment except appearance, and Best knew that in reality he and George R. were not at all alike.

He was sad about the man's horrible death, having been much taken with that friendly and ebullient gentleman. Of course, to most people's eyes all this mystery was just so much nonsense. Anyone could see it was just another robbery. The London, Chatham and Dover Railway, via Mr Cyril Bunting their sleek legal representative, were keen to rebut that assertion. This proved a struggle given that the victim's wallet and expensive jewellery were all missing: the solitaire diamond ring, gold and diamond cravat pin and the watch which had caught Best's attention when he had kept consulting it on the home-bound journey.

Bunting was even driven to asserting that there was no way of telling whether the man had ever been on the train at all. Best knew that it was scarcely likely that he *had not* boarded the train straight from the ferry but, if he hadn't, surely it was even stranger that his body should be found near the LCD railway track.

Maybe, thought Best, I should have warned him about displaying such wealth while travelling on our railways? The idea made him feel ashamed.

One could tell by his strained expression that Charlie Briggs, the guard on the Dover to London express on that fateful day, knew he was in an unenviable position. It was in his nature to be honest and straightforward but his employers just as clearly wanted him not to be.

He could not, he said, be absolutely certain that a man answering Mr Hardinge's description had been on the train that day, which was not surprising, given the number and assortment of passengers he had to deal with. That answer clearly satisfied Bunting. But then, under pressure from the coroner, he did agree that he was pretty certain that he could well have seen such a person at some time during that period. The man's description seemed familiar.

After a whispered consultation with Bunting he added that this sighting, if there was one, might easily have been on the way *out* to Dover, not necessarily on the return.

He described the state in which he found the first-class compartment that evening, and when the coroner enquired whether he agreed with the conclusion that this had been due to a drunken brawl, said carefully, 'I thought it might be.'

The coroner fixed him in the eye and reminded him that he was on oath, at which he blanched. Dr Washman then enquired just how bad the scene had been.

'Very bloody,' admitted Charlie Briggs, avoiding Bunting's eye, 'and there were white bits in it.'

'Bone?'

'Could have been.'

'Were you really of the opinion at the time that all this blood was merely the result of fisticuffs?'

Briggs looked about him desperately and saw Bunting looking at him warningly. Dr Washman saw it too and gave *him* a look which said don't you dare to intimidate my witnesses and do not imagine that you big city lawyers can come down here and try to pull the wool over the eyes of us simple country folk.

'You needn't be afraid of being honest,' he told Briggs. 'It is true that your company's reputation may suffer if it is found that a murder occurred on one of their trains but this will be as naught, I assure you, compared with the contempt which will be heaped upon them should it be suspected that they are trying to hide the truth or to intimidate one of my witnesses.'

Good for him, cheered Best. The man was almost as impressive as the brave and honest Dr Wakely, the London coroner famous for not allowing any interference in his cases. They wouldn't dare sack Briggs now.

'I thought that that amount of blood must be from a stabbing or a shooting,' Briggs said in a rush then coloured up.

Dr Washman nodded. 'Thank you, Mr Briggs. You may stand down now.'

The surgeon, a man in late middle age who wore the signs of a fondness for alcohol on his puce and blotchy countenance, was clearly a little out of his depth in such a case but his evidence was straightforward. The victim had been stabbed, four times. He had also suffered a blow to his head. He had probably died from loss of blood and shock. How long he had been dead was difficult to establish seeing as how the weather had been so cold and the body would have been frozen, then thawed, then partially refrozen.

It was possible that the knife found by the track could have been one of the weapons used. Some of the wounds had been caused by a similar double-edged knife. But he could not be absolutely certain that it was one of the murder weapons. He had obviously been reading the matter up in some textbooks because he began to explain how the size of the cut might differ from the width of the blade because skin was elastic and could close up slightly. If the point was sharp but the edges quite blunt the difference might be even more marked. What he was sure about was that there had been two weapons.

All that was left was for the jury to deliver their verdict.

Three things were on Best's mind during the proceedings. Why was such a wealthy man travelling without a manservant? What had happened to his luggage? He must have had some. Small keys had been found in his pocket but no tickets to suggest it had been left somewhere. And were the two men who had entered his compartment at Chatham implicated in some way?

He did not mention these matters partly because there was no evidence against the two men, apart from the fact one was hatless and both appeared flustered, and partly because if they were implicated, he didn't want to alert them.

Inquests were a problem for the police. So much vital information was revealed during the proceedings which was then spread far and wide by the newspapers. They didn't just report on it, either. They pontificated on its meaning and offered opinions as to the guilt or innocence and the honesty or duplicity of the witnesses and suspects. In doing so, as well as muddying the waters, they often aided the guilty, sometimes irreparably.

Should he later be accused of withholding evidence from the coroner he would claim that he had only just remembered about the two men. He had thought they had merely been running for a train. As well they might have been. After all, he reassured himself, the verdict would not have been any different had he shared this information with the court: 'Murder by person or persons unknown.'

Eighteen

It was a curious experience for Best to present himself at such monumental Tudor gates, thirty miles from home, and to be greeted by the familiar figure of a smartly helmeted London policeman.

The PC carefully inspected Best's warrant card then gave him a grin and a salute and said, 'Nice to see you down here, sir,' before ushering him into the small city that was Chatham Dockyard.

The Metropolitan Police had taken over the policing of the Royal Naval dockyards in 1860 after it was realized that to employ local people and even dockyard workers to do the job had not been a good idea. They were naturally susceptible to the influences of former colleagues, friends and even their own families. It wasn't only ships' stores and equipment that had gone missing, even items as large and heavy as anchors could be made to disappear with disconcerting ease.

Consequently, many single young London

constables expecting to spend their service in the fog-bound, bustling capital found themselves gazing out over docks as far away as Plymouth in Devon or Pembroke in South Wales. In comparison, Best realized, Chatham must seem almost a home posting, situated as it was on the River Medway, which led out into the Thames estuary.

Before coming to the dockyard Best had questioned the station master and ticket collector at Chatham railway station to find out if anyone recalled the two men who had rushed to catch the Continental express on that fateful evening. Unsurprisingly, they did not. As well as the time gap there was the fact that ticket collectors were too busy checking tickets for forgeries to register passengers' faces as well.

'Busy time of day,' the station master had said.

'Working men, farmers or sailors?' The ticket collector shrugged. 'Come through in their dozens.'

'On the express?' Best asked. Express train tickets were more expensive than standard local trains, and much more than the fares on the workmen's trains.

'Yes ... sometimes.' He shrugged again and turned away.

Obviously some kind of local arrangement was operating with the collusion of the ticket collectors but Best was not interested in catching small swindlers.

Next he had tried the cab drivers, who were obliged to look more closely at their passengers lest they were drunk or likely to decamp without paying their fares or even to rob them, particular hazards in a town not only awash with sailors but with its own army barracks. There would also be some desperate civilians about as the dockyard expansion wound down and men were suddenly thrown out of work. But, according to the gatehouse policeman, there were still almost four thousand men working in Chatham Dockyard.

Many of these had been taken on when the expansion began in 1865, after it had been realized that sailing ships were not enough and that Britain now needed an iron-clad 'steam navy', particularly as the French were building up such a fleet. For this purpose, convicts and workmen had been employed to drain more swampy ground and build three large non-tidal basins and four new dry docks as well as more factories and warehouses. In addition, there were the sailors, housed not very happily on old ships' hulks out in the river. He sighed. Needle in a haystack.

He was surprised by the elegant air of the buildings just inside the dockyard entrance.

Directly ahead of him was a substantial Georgian church topped incongruously by a tiny circle of slender columns supporting a small dome and a weather vane. To his immediate right was a single-storey white colonnaded building, the Guard House, where he had been told he would find the dockyard police, including Detective Sergeant Hanwell.

Best had had dealings with Hanwell when the man was a detective constable on C Division. He had found him to be a good, workaday police officer, any lack of education or high intelligence being more than compensated for by his sheer enthusiasm for the job and native nose for villains. Best recalled him being constantly on the lookout for thieves and fraudsters – with the result that he caught a good many.

Despite protestations that he was happy with his lot, Hanwell was clearly delighted to see a fellow detective from the Great Smoke. He shook Best's hand heartily, grasping his arm with the other in a painful grip.

Hanwell was a man of considerable proportions, the kind one could see working over a blacksmith's forge, his huge muscles rippling, beads of sweat standing out on his broad brow as he bent metal to his will, rather than poring over files in a cramped and stuffy CID office.

His powerful image must be useful to him in a dockyard but he made no attempt to resemble a manual worker. His curled brim bowler was well brushed as was his high-fastening single-breasted black suit. But, as so often with burly men, he gave the impression that his clothes constrained him and that at any minute he might burst out of them.

'Plenty of work 'ere,' he confided to Best. 'Mostly thievery, of course. We've even 'ad men stealing each other's tools, which makes it 'ard to keep the peace between 'em. Don't take much to stir up violence here. An' we come in for plenty ourselves.' Best had heard that when patrolling, the dock police were instructed always to keep each other in sight.

'Many Irish?'

'Oh, aye. Plenty. But they're no particular bother except when they're in their cups.' He grinned knowingly. 'No bombs, yet.'

'Should hope not.'

The thought of the damage Fenians could do to Her Majesty's navy at Chatham was appalling and not only with exploding coal. And there obviously were some sympathizers out here. Quite recently three cases of dynamite had been found among the incoming goods at Queenborough. But what could the authorities do when the Irish were so much part of the workforce? Fortunately, many of the Irish in Britain were against the dynamite campaign, not only because they were reluctant to kill their neighbours but they were aware that the backlash against them could be serious. All very well, some of them said, for Fenians talking about killing the Queen when they are back in the safety of America.

Hanwell listened patiently to Best's embarrassingly sparse description of his two railway companions. Why didn't I take more notice at the time, he thought, instead of being so preoccupied with Fenians and phylloxera?

'One of the men had a slight cast in his eye,' he added hopefully, 'and the other, the shorter and darker one, was missing the two top joints of his middle fingers. Can't remember which hand.'

Hanwell grunted and continued looking at him, expecting more.

'Does that bring any pair to mind?' Best asked eventually.

'Hmm.' Hanwell grimaced and rubbed his right hand over his fleshy chin where, despite close shaving, dark stubble was threatening to break through. 'Not off hand. The cast in the eye. Bit common that, of course.'

Best nodded. That was true.

'And a lot of the fellows 'ere 'ave fingers missing and the like,' said Hanwell. 'In a place like this, with all this machinery around– ' he shrugged – 'you know what it's like?'

Best did. He had once sent out wanted notices for a mechanic who had no left thumb. He had been deluged with messages offering one-thumbed suspects, some with the right thumb missing.

'Look,' said Hanwell standing up, 'why don't you go and 'ave a wander around, see if you can see any likely blokes. I'll take you down there then I'll go off and have a word with one or two of me mates – an' take a look in me files.' He pointed a thick finger at his forehead, screwed it, and grinned. 'See what I can come up with. Can't always bring 'em to mind straight away. You know 'ow it is.' Best certainly did. 'Got to do a bit of dredging first, 'aven't you?'

'Right.' Working by the water was clearly affecting the man's vocabulary.

As they walked down the hill the sights and sounds of the docks, the belching chimneys and the endless noise, began to overwhelm Best. Hanwell seemed impervious to it.

'That's the longest brick building in Europe,' he said pointing proudly at the hemp-spinning shed and ropery from which came overwhelming pounding and rattling. 'It's a quarter of a mile in length.'

At the bottom of the hill was a large

Georgian mansion, the residence of the Admiral Superintendent, and a two-storey row of brick buildings crowned with a clock tower that would not have been out of place in any small town square. Peeping over the top of them was the Officers' Terrace, a row of handsome four-storey dwellings where the rest of the dockyard élite lived.

Contrasting very oddly with this peaceful urbanity was the frantic, noisy, industrial scene opposite and beyond where lay the Smithery, the Mast House, the Wheelwrights' Shops and the slips in which ships were under construction. Steam hammers thumped, the punching and sheering machines punched and sheered, the saw mills ground their way through planks of oak and the clanking and whistling trains constantly traversed the huge dockyard.

Best realized how easy it would be to be distracted by all this noise and activity and not notice what was happening nearby. He put his hands over his ears and screwed up his face.

Hanwell grinned at him. 'You get used to it,' he shouted.

He went off to consult with the uniformed constables while Best wandered over to the nearest slips where the hulks of two new ships were being completed. Both were ironclad steam and sail warships. Workmen swarmed all over them, hammering, riveting, caulking, forging and armouring.

As with most such endeavours, to the outsider it looked chaotic. How could anyone possibly know what was going on? What was the overall plan?

He watched, hypnotized, for a while then wandered over to the riverside where, stretching out from the land into the water, was a line of hulks and depot ships joined together, each topped, incongruously, with a wooden roof.

The wind was wild and ferocious. 'Bracing', as the east-coast holiday resorts described their weather. Here, with the flat open waters of the Medway providing little impediment, breezes quickly became gales. Even the few seagulls looked ruffled by its wildness.

Two ships stood off in the river. Fussing around between them were several smaller craft including a rowing boat manned by members of the water police in their flat caps. They, too, were members of the Metropolitan Police, who patrolled around the marsh islands and up the Medway's narrow inlets and meandering creeks to prevent theft, smuggling, unlawful landing and fishing too close to the docks and, as unlikely as it seemed, to keep a look out for the enemy. No one here forgot that, way back in 1667, the Dutch fleet had sneaked into the Thames and sailed up the Medway, destroyed several fine ships and captured the flagship, the *Royal Charles*. It was the Royal Navy's most humiliating defeat.

Turning his back to the river he saw the bulky figure of Hanwell coming towards him, hand raised. Best met him halfway.

'I think I've got something,' he announced. 'One of the constables remembers a pair who were done for thieving from luggage and picking pockets on the London to Chatham,' said Hanwell. 'Edgehill and Simpson are their names. Edgehill has some injury to his right hand, he says. Joints missing, he thinks. He can't remember whether the other one had a squint in his eye because he wasn't allowed back here.'

Best frowned. 'And Edgehill was? He was taken on again?'

Hanwell shrugged and said, 'He's an anchorsmith,' as though that were all the explanation that were necessary.

'So...?' Best was puzzled. They were paying skilled men off, engineers and joiners, but a blacksmith who was a known thief had been re-employed? No wonder they had workmen stealing from each other.

'Anchorsmiths are as rare as snowballs in the tropics,' Hanwell explained. 'Can't get 'em. Have you seen what it's like in there?'

He nodded towards No. 1 Smithery. 'Hot as hell, noisy as bedlam and bloody hard graft – them anchors can weigh over seventy-two hundredweight. The smiths have to work twelve hours a day, cos of the furnaces. They has to comb the country to get them. Then they pay them the highest wages of all the skilled men and give 'em eight pints of strong beer a day – just to keep 'em. So...' he spread his hands wide, 'even if they are naughty lads, criminals even, they can some-times get back in when they've done their time.'

'He's here now, this Edgehill?' Best asked eagerly, glancing towards the Smithery.

Hanwell shook his head. 'No. He's up at St Mary's Island.' St Mary's Island was the series of swampy mudflats to the north which had been drained to make the dock-yard extension.

Young PC Acland led Best up there. They crossed a wide bridge which took them into another warren of dry docks, wet docks, warehouses, factories and boiler and mach-ine shops between which steam cranes and steam trains lifted and ferried mountains of wood and iron and out of which came relentless pounding, thudding, banging, hammering, jingling and jangling.

Acland, too, pointed out all the different docks and buildings like a proud father who

155

had watched this infant project grow to its present almost completed state. Best, intent on catching his prey, only half listened. He was excited that he might be within grasp and the constant noise seemed to prevent his mind from working properly. At last they stopped before another smithery. 'In there,' Acland said.

The wall of heat that met them as they went in almost stopped Best's breath. He had never felt anything like it. Was this what it was like in the tropics? If so, he could never survive there.

'He's out at the back,' said a leather-aproned workman as he pulled a molten rod out of the furnace and held it up before him as if in admiration.

They went through to the back and looked around outside. No sign of Edgehill. Acland suddenly pointed to a figure in the distance. 'There he is.'

The man was walking towards them. When he saw Acland pointing at him he halted abruptly, looked around, turned and ran.

Best and Acland took off in pursuit but Acland was not only younger and fitter, he knew his ground. Bounding ahead, he dodged around a massive steam crane which lay in their path and jumped over a pile of planks Best had not even seen.

The chase was long and hard and at the

end of it Best had to admit that he was lost. He stood quite alone beside the wall which encircled the site, gazed down into the murky waters of the River Medway, then back towards the dockyard buildings.

There, coming towards him, breathless but triumphant was young Acland with Edgehill in tow. The blacksmith must have been much stronger than the PC, honed as he was by his daily exertions, but he was even more breathless. Obviously, slaving over a hot furnace was not good for the lungs.

As they drew nearer Best's heart began to sink. He was loath to disappoint the constable after such heroic exertion but when they arrived he had to admit, 'It's not him.'

'Oh, never mind,' said Acland. 'He's obviously done *something*, hasn't he!'

Nineteen

'We have to find out whether one of our important informants has been eliminated recently,' said Best.

Williamson shrugged. 'I tried to get that out of Anderson. But you know what he's like.'

Best nodded. 'Likes to be king of the castle.'

Well-connected, Dublin-born, Robert Anderson was a vain little man but a great opportunist. He had seized his chance when as a young government solicitor in Dublin he had been handed the wealth of Fenian intelligence assiduously collected from informants by the British Consul in New York. His task was to collate it and reach conclusions on the present state of the Fenian movement.

He had promptly eradicated the names of the informants from these reports, allotting them nom de plumes instead. One of the most important was known as Informant M. From this material he wrote a report and with these bricks he built himself a kingdom. He became *the* expert. The informants now reported to him alone. Consequently, when the country became panicked over the Clerkenwell Explosion he was brought over to London to act as secretary and adviser to the Home Office's new special committee on Irish matters.

As Fenian activity died down the new department disbanded but Anderson stayed on at the Home Office on the substantial salary of £50 a month. Now, with the Fenians' rebirth, albeit under several titles, the Home Office anti-Fenian committee had been reborn as well and Williamson, as head of the Yard's new Special Irish Branch, was obliged to call on them every day to absorb their words of wisdom. Anderson let out dribs and drabs of information gathered from his informants and excerpts from Clan na Gael circulars.

The police did appreciate why Anderson was so careful about the informants' identities. Lord Mayo, the Chief Secretary for Ireland, had talked about an informant when dining at the Vice-regal Lodge in Dublin. The conversation was overheard by a waiter and the traitor was duly murdered on his arrival in New York. Nonetheless, the police felt that Anderson could be a little more helpful with them instead of guarding his own fiefdom so assiduously. After all, they were on the front line.

'He won't even tell the Home Secretary their names,' said Williamson. Best thought that very sensible. 'But he did let me have this.' Williamson pushed a piece of paper over his desk. It was an excerpt from a recent Clan na Gael circular with two chilling lines underlined in red ink:

> You will note with pleasure that the informer is foredoomed, that no man can betray and live, no corner of the earth is too obscure or too far to hide.

'Oh, and he did confirm that Georgia is in one of the Clan's sixteen US districts.'

'Surely he could tell you whether one of his informants has been killed lately?'

Williamson shook his head. 'He said that as far as he knew none have. But then said that he wouldn't necessarily know yet or tell me if they had because if it got out it would confirm the Fenians' suspicions and maybe endanger that informant's contacts.'

'Wonderful,' said Best, exasperated. 'So how am I supposed to find out if George R. was a Fenian informer?'

'You still think he was?'

'I've no idea.' Best stared out of the window into the foggy courtyard and men's urinal below. 'But he *was* behaving quite strangely on the ship, as if he was wary of something. And he deliberately avoided travelling back on the train with me.'

Williamson smiled. 'Could it have been your cologne, Ernest?'

'Impossible!' laughed Best.

They contemplated the problem in silence for a moment or two. Then Best said, 'Well, I will have to go to the usual places for information on American citizens' – the American Embassy and the American Club – 'and then...' He paused. 'I'd better go and see O'Brien again.'

A thinner and even paler O'Brien sat eating his ordinary in his usual solitary state by the fire in the Printers' Arms.

As Best came in he glanced up and a smile instantly lit his face transforming it from solid potato to almost puckish but then it froze quickly when he realized the implications of Best's arrival. Not only must I remind him of something he'd rather forget, that he was a traitor, thought Best, but he thinks I must want something more from him. And I do.

Best liked the man so he decided there and then that he would make this current errand quick and painless and explain that the information he had given him about forthcoming Fenian plans had told the police nothing they did not already know. That should relieve him of some of his guilt and, hopefully, lessen his fear of reprisal.

'You cannot keep away from work after all, then, Ernest?' O'Brien called over, managing to inject a casually jovial tone into his voice.

Best shook his head. 'Just passing and thought I'd drop in to console my old friends who have to work for a living.'

He paid much attention to the other customers and the landlord and even the new barmaid, who he treated as a fresh acquaintance before he strolled over to O'Brien with his pint in hand. The pantomime was necessary. O'Brien might be being watched.

As he was exchanging pleasantries with the Irish compositor it dawned on him how delicate was the task he was about to perform – enquiring of one informer whether any other prominent informer had recently been murdered.

He asked just the same, after a decent interval.

O'Brien blanched, his hand tightening on his knife and fork while fear and despair etched itself onto his face. He looked as if he might cry. It was obvious he thought that the authorities Best had passed his information on to were not going to let him go but to keep on using him, again and again.

'I think you must have realized that I am a police officer, and the reason I need to know,' said Best quickly, 'it is just to help me solve a case. You'll have heard of the murder of an American on the London, Chatham and Dover Railway – well, I met him on the way back from France. The thing is I just don't know *why* he was killed. It could have just been robbery – or he might have been a prominent Fenian.' He cleared his throat. 'An informer. All I want to know is whether I'm looking in the right direction. I'm not expecting you to divulge any real secrets.' Well, if you're not, he thought, you should be. You're getting soft and you've no right to be. 'It would be a great help to me if you could tell me,' he continued then added quickly, 'By the way, the information you gave me in Paris was already known to us. So you need not feel guilty.'

As he had hoped, the Irishman's face relaxed a little. He released his tight grip on his knife and fork and lowered them onto his plate.

'I won't come to you again,' Best promised. Was he going mad? This man was involved with dangerous people. What's the matter with me? he thought. But he already knew. What was the matter was that he was in sympathy with their aims and realized that they weren't just murderous thugs but a people fighting for their freedom – just as the Italians had recently been forced to do. Being half Italian he had cheered them on. In any case, he sensed that O'Brien's usefulness as an informant, always limited, was now finished. He only hoped that the man wasn't personally.

O'Brien took a deep breath, pulled out his watch and stared at it and, as he did so, he said, without looking up or turning his head, 'I've heard that there was a plan to eliminate,' he stumbled over the word, 'to eliminate a traitor. Someone they thought might have told the police about the Birmingham bomb factory.' He replaced the watch in his pocket and turned to Best and said, 'But I haven't heard what happened, if anything. Nor who he was.'

'I see.'

'We're being much more careful about information these days. So much has got out.' He looked miserable but carried on. 'They're thinking that the fewer of us who know the details the better.' He paused and took a deep breath. 'I'm not being told much.'

Best believed him. 'That's sensible. The more who know, the more danger of it getting out,' he said, trying to comfort him but probably making it worse.

The joke was that the Birmingham bomb

factory had not been betrayed by an informer. It had been found quite accidentally
because Irishmen were purchasing such
industrial quantities of nitric acid and
glycerine, the latter purportedly 'for hair-
dressing preparations', that the chemist
became suspicious and had the good sense
to inform the police.

Oh, well, that was that. He lifted his glass
to the Irishman and said goodbye.

And still it continued, the usual endless flow
of letters they received following a murder
and which grew in volume if the murder
remained unsolved for any length of time.

As ever, the missives were full of helpful
suggestions and advice. Advice as to which
path to follow, which clue was obvious to all
but the police, which type of person was
likely to commit this type of crime, obvious,
again, to all but the police. Or they simply
insisted that they had vital information that
they could not risk putting in a letter but
must pass on personally.

'The Railway Murder' or 'the Murder on
the Continental Express' encouraged all of
these and more involving, as it did, so many
dramatic elements: a wealthy foreign victim
travelling first class on a Continental express
as well as more proof of the dangers of railway travel. Yet again, the victim had been

thrown onto the track like so much litter.

The fact that he was American brought forth extra suggestions as to motive. Might it be due to still simmering resentments following their Civil War? Perhaps the victim had killed someone's son or raped their wife during the conflict? Or afterwards been one of those to take advantage of the ruined South?

The commissioner always insisted that they take these letters seriously to reassure the public and on the grounds that, occasionally, they were sent by genuine witnesses or others with real information to impart. Very occasionally, they were.

Usually, however, they were a complete waste of precious time. Particularly when the detectives were obliged to follow them up in case the writer really had that important information to which they laid claim. Most often this turned out to be nonsense and the writer to be one of the many deluded drawn to stories of crime. Heaven knows enough lunatics turned up at police stations without them having to go out looking for more!

Such resentments churned about in Best's mind as he paused halfway through a not-even-promising pile of letters. He fell to staring out of the window idly watching the poor constable who had been allotted the thankless task of guarding the gentlemen's urinal in case some wild-eyed Irishman or Irish-American should deposit his bombs there. Best wondered how was he supposed to divine this if the man did not speak nor draw attention to himself by looking evil and shifty. At least, he thought returning to his letters, this task was preferable to manning a fixed post outside a public lavatory.

As he began reading the second from last in his pile he perked up. This one looked at least promising. It was written on Athenaeum Club paper in a hand halfway between the scrawl of an aristocrat or other similar man of substance and the copperplate of the office clerk who was so often given the task of transcribing the aforesaid scrawl into legibility. It began:

Sir,
    I am uncertain whether this information will be of use to you.

Well, that was a good start. Humility and uncertainty were rare ingredients in such missives. It continued:

I was boarding the London, Chatham and Dover Railway Continental express at Chatham on the same day that the American gentleman was attacked, when I saw two men, Frenchmen I think they were. They alighted from a first-class carriage in the Victoria-bound part of the train. One of them stopped me and enquired in broken English if I could tell them which were the carriages which would be branching off for the City. (They did not ask that in so many words, we communicated in a mixture of signs, gesticulations, my poor French and their odd words of barely coherent English.)

The encounter was all very hurried owing to the imminent departure of the train, but I do recall being surprised when they got into a second-class carriage. Thinking about it later it was more surprising that they should have been travelling first class initially because they looked rather dishevelled, poorly dressed and a little wild-eyed. Of course it could be that my imagination has coloured this description since learning of the dreadful fate of the American gentleman.

Should you wish to discuss the above matter you will find me at the above club most afternoons. Failing that, please leave a note there stating when it would be convenient for us to meet.

Yours faithfully,
Harold Coates

What an exemplary witness. And how extraordinary that another pair of suspicious men
had been seen exchanging carriages. Of,
course it was possible that his two, after all,
might merely have been boarding at Chatham not changing compartments having
murdered George R. Or, then again, maybe
four men had attacked poor George R. That
was a dreadful thought. But Mr Coates
thought these two were French! That confused matters.

Had the Fenians brought French thugs
with them to help do the dirty deed? It
would be a good cover and a new departure
for them. Certainly the French seemed very
happy for Fenians to plot in Paris but he
didn't know of Frenchmen who were
actually involved themselves.

Or were they French thieves – or merely
confused aliens? As for the possibility of the
murderers changing onto the City-bound
carriages, which divided off at Herne Hill,
that had never even occurred to him. He
chided himself that this was because he was
so set on the fact that the two men in his
compartment must be the culprits.

It was all very confusing but at least he
now had something new to work on. The
exercise had proved more helpful than
anticipated. He stood up, reached for his

overcoat and was about to leave for the Athenaeum in nearby St James's when a young constable put his head around the door.

'Someone downstairs asking for you. Says he is a good friend of your Yankee.'

Twenty

George R.'s London friend was also an American but a much less colourful one. A soft-voiced Bostonian, Joseph C. Herbert peered at Best through disconcertingly thick-lensed spectacles. He appeared to be extremely shocked by the fate which had overtaken his friend and quite at a loss to explain it.

'I don't understand it,' he kept saying. 'I'm sure he hadn't an enemy in the world. He was such a friendly, jovial man. How could anyone do this to him?' The pale, myopic eyes looked bewildered. 'I don't understand it.'

'Neither do I,' admitted Best. 'But we will find out,' he added with a confidence he didn't feel.

According to Mr Herbert, George R.

Hardinge was exactly who he had said he was and a reluctant participant in the American Civil War on the Confederate side. He had been wounded in a battle during which he had distinguished himself by his bravery. In subsequent civilian life he was also, according to Herbert, exactly who he had said he was. That is, the owner of a vine nursery in Georgia anxious to assist the French in saving their vineyards.

'He wasn't profiteering from their situation?' Many were, Best had heard.

Herbert was affronted. 'Oh I'm sure not! I'm sure not! In fact,' he added sadly, 'George always said that the wine trade without the French would be like a bird without wings. Of course, he *did* think it was a good thing that countries like Algeria and Spain were expanding their trade to help fill the gap in the market and he assisted them where he could.'

It occurred to Best that this pale, wispy-haired soul was an odd kind of friend for the ebullient George R. 'You were friends in America?'

'Oh no. I met him at Kew Gardens, where I was studying botany. He came to find out what they could tell him about phylloxera.'

'Did he have Irish friends in London?'

Herbert looked perplexed by this seemingly unconnected question. He shook his

171

head as though clearing the cobwebs from his mind and rocked back and forward a little in his chair. 'Not that I know of,' he said eventually. 'I mean he *might* have ... I never saw him with anyone else and when we were together we discussed viticulture and horti-culture.'

'So, in fact,' said Best slowly, 'what you know about him is only what he told you?'

'Er ... Yes,' Herbert nodded, puzzled again by the drift of the conversation. Then he seemed to grasp the implication of Best's question and said, 'No, wait a minute. About him being a brave Confederate and wound-ed – that was something *another* friend of mine told me. He had also been a Confeder-ate soldier and knew of George by repute.'

'And this friend's name is?'

'Henry Makepeace.'

'And his address?'

'Oh, I'm afraid he's gone back home – to the United States.'

Best sighed inwardly. Two steps forward, one step back.

The dynamite hysteria had been reignited despite all information received being acted upon and a watch being kept on ports, particularly Liverpool, to prevent explosives being sneaked into the country. Despite also an Act being rushed through Parliament making it a felony for anyone to possess explosives for unlawful purposes.

Notwithstanding all these precautions and, indeed, making all of them appear futile, five slabs of Atlas Powder 'A', dynamite of American make, had been found lying in the Primrose Hill tunnel of the London and North Western railway line. Oddly, they were not attached to a fuse or detonator, so the presumption was that they had been hidden there, or thrown away by a conspirator either frightened of being caught in possession or nervous that they might explode of their own volition.

In truth, more 'outrages' had been expected for some time. Unbridled threats were being made in the dynamite press and at the Fenian Conventions. Matters discussed included the signing of a mutual-aid treaty with Britain's enemy, Russia, the supply of officers to assist the Boers in their struggle against Britain and the acquisition of hand grenades, arms and even cannon for use against targets on the mainland and in Ireland come the revolution and the assassination of Queen Victoria.

The authorities had been warned that no fewer than six Fenian dynamitards had entered the country during the last year. Their first attempt had been the October underground bombing. Now, it seemed, they planned more attacks on the railways and these were virtually impossible to defend. Adding more menace to their 'fiendish devices' was the fact that O'Donovan Rossa's crudely fashioned, gunpowder-filled bombs had given way to the more sophisticated Clan-made variety filled with dynamite.

Given this situation, it was only by emphasizing the possible Fenian connection to the George R. murder, which in fact he was beginning to doubt, that Best was allowed the time to go to the Athenaeum Club in Pall Mall.

It wasn't far: out of Great Scotland Yard, into Whitehall, through the Horse Guards gate opposite and their parade ground which skirted the eastern edge of St James's Park then across The Mall. From here, he climbed the Duke of York steps, which were guarded at the top by the man himself on a pillar built high enough, it was claimed, for him to escape his creditors.

Ahead of him was Waterloo Place. The Athenaeum occupied a prime site on the south-west side at the junction with Pall Mall and was first in a whole row of gentlemen's clubs.

As though to advertise the superior erudition of *its* members, the Athenaeum's exterior was a hymn to ancient Greece from the club's stately portico, Parthenon frieze and the statue of Athena, Goddess of Wisdom, Industry and War, who stood guard over the entrance. Nonetheless, to Best's taste the building was a little plain, stark and stolid.

The Grecian theme, he noticed, continued inside where ivory-white columns supported the hall's wagon roof and a mosaic floor led to where the grand staircase took flight. He didn't manage to see much more, the porter smartly directing him first right into the morning room. Here, ensconced in a leather library chair, by a roaring fire, he found Mr Harold Coates.

The tone of the man's letter had suggested an odd mixture of precise common sense, humility and confidence and Best had wondered whether he would live up to this image.

Mr Coates turned out to be a bright-eyed, cheerful man who jumped up to welcome Best cordially. His conversational style resembled that of his letter in one respect, alternating as it did between deeply thoughtful, slow pronouncements and boyishly eager bursts of rapid speech which often qualified or corrected his previous statement.

They kept their voices low in deference to the many gentlemen who had their heads buried behind the daily papers in what was also 'the newspaper room'.

When asked for a description of the two men he had helped transfer to the City-bound carriages Coates went into a reverie, steepling his hands up to his lips.

'Why, for example, did you think they were French?' prompted Best.

'Well, I wasn't sure. But I thought they might be. Well, afterwards I did. At that moment I was too busy trying to communicate and I tried French because I realized that they must be foreign.'

'Why was that?'

He sat forward, elbows on knees. 'Er, let me see. It was their lively facial expression, raised eyebrows and excitable hand movements – all that kind of thing. Definitely not English. Then, of course, there was their clothes. They looked foreign and rather rural and they had weathered complexions.'

'And physically?'

'Oh, they were middle-sized, both of them. Quite stocky, both of them, and dark haired, I think.'

'What sort of hats did they wear?'

'One wore a soft cap and the other was hatless. Oh, and...' his face lit up, 'one of them was holding one of those big clay pipes with a bowl in the shape of a head. This one was Queen Victoria's head. I was quite shocked by that.'

So was Best. He'd seen pipes with heads of Napoleon or Robespierre and even Wellington (with a French soldier on the stem thumbing his nose at him) but not, so far, Queen Victoria. He stopped Coates abruptly with an upraised hand. Where was it? Where had he seen something like that lately? Two men, one with one of those clay pipes in his hand? He shook his head. 'Sorry, go on.'

'That's it, really. Oh, except one had a large mole on his face.' He pointed up beside his own eye then paused and looked apologetic. 'It was all so quick, you see, and I was trying to help them but also make sure I caught the train myself and...'

'No need to apologize, you've been very helpful.' And he hadn't tried to embroider his statement when he realized it was a bit sparse. The imagination of some witnesses could take flight when excited because they were speaking to a Scotland Yard detective.

Best slapped his knee suddenly. 'Got it!'

Mr Coates looked up, startled.

'I saw them in the saloon on the ferry!'

'Oh.' His face lit up. 'How splendid.'

'They didn't look very lively then. Morose, in fact. But, then, it was quite a lively crossing!'

Twenty-One

'According to Mr Herbert, the man was who he claimed to be,' Best explained. 'So that means that George R. did have a legitimate reason for visiting France and so probably was not a Fenian after all.'

Cheadle pondered this statement, head back, eyes closed. It was a disconcerting habit of his particularly as, these days, one could never be certain whether in fact he had gone to sleep. However, on this occasion, he opened his eyes suddenly to ask, ' So 'ow do you know this Herbert fellow is who 'e says 'e is?'

'Er...' That had never occurred to him. I'm getting slow, he thought. Or perhaps just tired.

'Bit odd that this Coates bloke turns up at the same time as this Herbert fellow, ain't it?'

Best had to admit that it was.

'Could be trying to make us look the other way.'

Best nodded. Comment wasn't necessary

when Cheadle was in full flow.

'They could be Fenians themselves wanting to cover up their part in the murder. Send you off in another direction.'

Best was beginning to feel as if he were lost in a land of broken mirrors. Everywhere he looked images fractured and turned into something else.

He gave Cheadle's theory thoughtful consideration. He tried to envisage Herbert, the hesitant academic, and Coates, the painfully honest member of the most intellectually élite of London's clubs, as rabid revolutionaries before admitting, 'I can't really see either of them in that guise.'

At one time Cheadle would have picked him up for using 'fancy words' like guise, but now he shrugged his huge shoulders and said, 'Just don't count the Fenians out of the picture on their say so, that's all I'm saying. Those Fenians are wily buggers.'

A compliment from one wily old bugger to others.

'I won't,' Best assured him. 'I don't have much else to go on, anyway. I suppose.' he added morosely, 'George R. might have legitimate reasons for being in France and also be a Fenian.'

'Best cover.' Cheadle pushed himself up in his chair.

'But they usually want to advertise the

disposal of an informant or a supposed informant – as a warning to others.'

'Ah, yes.' He wagged his big sausage-like forefinger at Best. 'But they don't want any more of their men caught by us and hanged, do they? That don't look good neither, does it? Bad for recruitment.' He paused and pulled at his long side-whiskers. 'This could be a good sign. Mebbe they think you're gettin' too close.'

Well, they'd certainly be wrong about that, thought Best, I'm completely befogged.

'They'll be 'appy if you get them,' he said pointing upwards. 'They' or 'them' were always the bigwigs, the commissioner, idle civil servants at the Home Office or Members of Parliament.

'I'll go to the Ludgate Hill and Holborn Viaduct stations next, then on to the French quarters.'

They pondered this prospect for a few moments, both gazing out of the window at the comings and goings on the cab rank outside the Rising Sun public house opposite. Suddenly, Cheadle slapped his hand on his desk and said, 'Right, what's the picture if it is these Froggies what did it?' He liked to talk in pictures. 'Why would these Frenchies want to kill your friend?'

His friend. Wily old bugger had realized that that was how he felt about George R.

even though he hadn't put it into so many words in his own mind. There were so few bright and lively souls in this world they could ill afford to lose any, was how he saw it.

'Well, for money, of course. A lot of these wine growers are desperate just now so they might have accepted Fenian money to kill George R. There's plenty of it about.' Indeed it was regarded as a bit of a wry joke that some of the Fenians were living like lords in Paris. Only the best of everything for them – paid for by dollars and cents garnered from poor Irish immigrants in the US anxious to free their homeland from British tyranny and poverty. 'Or it could be just straightforward robbery due to the same desperation. Or...'

Cheadle waited. Finally he said, ' 'Ow about this disease Philly – whatever?'

Best drew his hand down over his tired face. 'I've thought about that. But I can't see how. He was trying to help them and...'

'Hmm,' said Cheadle, whose long experience as a police officer had left him with little faith in the charitable impulses of others. 'I'd look at this business a bit more closely if I were you,' he said.

'Right, I will,' Best agreed but wondered if anyone was going to allow him the time to do that.

Cheadle tapped his nose with his forefinger. 'In the meantime we won't tell no one it might not be Fenians that did it, will we?'

Best made his way from the claustrophobic confines of Scotland Yard down to the riverside, where he could at least see the sky. It was a murky and misty sky but the murk and mist did soften the outlines of the ugly wharves and factories on the opposite bank. On this side, the still-pristine Victoria Embankment stretched before him invitingly.

A pale winter sun was managing to filter through to catch at the glass in the handsome iron lamps which marched along the curving river wall and the edges of the somewhat sinister dolphins coiled around their feet.

He walked eastwards, passing under the massive Hungerford Bridge which carried the South-Eastern Railway over the river to its new West End terminus and hotel at Charing Cross. Crossing back from the riverside pavement he entered the Victoria Embankment Gardens, where already one or two worthies were commemorated in marble and stone: Robert Raikes, the founder of Sunday Schools and Helen's hero, and the philosopher and social reformer John Stuart Mill.

Best enjoyed the gardens but was sad to

see how the imposing Adelphi Terrace which had once lined the river bank was losing its glory now that it had been marooned so far inland. He could remember too when the Thames lapped up against the south terrace of Somerset House, surely the grandest of government buildings, which he passed shortly before crossing the boundary between Westminster and the capital's financial heart, the City of London.

He turned left by Blackfriars Bridge and walked up New Bridge Street. He came to a halt before a mildly Italianate edifice fashioned out of parti-coloured bricks and embellished with turrets and medieval arched windows: Ludgate Hill railway station.

During the early years of the railway mania a Royal Commission had decreed that no line should penetrate the centre of London. Thus it came to pass that London's termini formed a circle around the edges of the capital like claws grasping a precious gemstone. The ruling caused not only great inconvenience to passengers wishing to continue onwards but also more and more street congestion as the passengers, their luggage and all manner of freight piled onto growlers, omnibuses and vans to make the journey across the great divide.

Oddly, it was the ever-struggling-to-survive

London, Chatham and Dover Railway which was not only the first to venture over the Thames into the City of London but also the first to meet up with a line from the Northern grouping of termini via the Metropolitan Railway, the world's first underground passenger railway.

One of the reasons cited for allowing this encroachment into the City of London was that the LCDR line was needed to carry farm produce to the Farringdon and Newgate Markets and to stop the unsavoury practice of driving animals across London Bridge. A lattice-girder bridge carrying four LCDR tracks had been flung across the River Thames and, as if to celebrate its cheeky encroachment, flanked at each end by a huge and highly decorative LCDR coat of arms emblazoned with the bravura motto 'Invicta'.

Monumental viaducts carried the rails onwards leaving little money to build Ludgate Hill Station, the city terminus of the Continental express. Not surprisingly this soon proved inadequate and was superseded by another terminus further on, Holborn Viaduct, reached by an extension of the railway viaduct which to the fury of many managed to spoil the eastward view of St Paul's Cathedral in the process.

Best's quarry might have alighted at either

one of these two stations. He did not expect much help at either and got none. Too much time had elapsed since these unprepossessing foreign gentlemen arrived in the capital. Had they even been noticed at the time they were unlikely to remain alive in the memories of porters, who were constantly seeking prosperous passengers, or busy ticket collectors and cab drivers.

Best was given some hope, however, by the Holborn Viaduct station master, who assured him that the guard on the City section of that LCDR train was an observant character and that should he respond to Best's description of the two foreign men he would immediately telegraph the Yard. Buoyed up by such unusual cooperation, Best left Holborn Viaduct and headed for his last port of call for that day.

The light was fading fast and the lamplighters were out in force by the time he reached the newly constructed Holborn Circus where an equestrian Prince Albert raised his hat to the City of London oblivious to the chaotic evening traffic whirling about him. A short way along Holborn he turned left down historic Fetter Lane, which had given shelter to several famous people from John Dryden to Thomas Paine as well as two murderesses and numerous religious Nonconformists. Several tiny, almost secret

185

alleyways led off to Inns of Court and chapels. Further south one could hardly miss the massive new mock-Tudor Public Record Office, the national repository for state and law records.

Crossing Fleet Street he entered the alleyway that led to Mitre Court and the accommodation address for replies to G.C.'s newspaper pleas. There he left a letter requesting a meeting with her.

Back in Fleet Street the air was growing chill and damp but the cheerfully blazing gaslights, trained on the little shop windows which nestled between newspaper offices and banks, lit up displays of Bibles and law books, expensive shirts for expensive barristers, stationery for their chambers and gloves for their well-manicured hands.

A grotesque sight brought Best's long stride to an abrupt halt. Displayed on outstretched wooden hands that almost seemed to be waving were a pair of chamois-leather gloves – just like those worn by George R.

Above them, illuminated by the street lamp, his own reflection. Rawston was right – he did look like the American. He was about the same height as George R. – a little above average, dark hair, similar sideburns and a dark jacket set off by a colourful, decorative waistcoat.

Of course no Englishman would confuse

them. But, his heart almost stopped as a terrible thought struck him, a foreigner might.

Oh, God! He was killed in mistake for me!

Twenty-Two

Best could not shake himself free from the idea that George R. had been murdered by the Fenians in mistake for him. He reminded himself that so far the Fenians had only killed one policeman, and that – they claimed – had been an accident when they had blown off the bolt of the Manchester police van during the rescue of two of their members. But there had been constant threats against them, and, with the recent disposal of informers, they had shown they meant business. He found the thought utterly depressing.

He turned over and over in his mind the questions why they might have confused George R. with him and why they should want to kill him anyway.

His contact with O'Brien was the obvious answer. Had the man confessed to them what he had done? Or had he given himself away somehow? He had seemed nervous in that Montmartre restaurant as though he expected trouble any minute and was very relieved when Best told him he was no longer going to meet him at the Printers' Arms.

Of course, it might be that the Fenians had noted Best's friendship with the printer and decided to kill him to prevent O'Brien letting down his guard and passing on vital information, not even realizing that he had done so already.

It had been foolish, he acknowledged, to send him to make contact with O'Brien in the first place. Scotland Yard detectives were too well known to stay unnoticed for long.

But how had the confusion between him and the American come about?

It was obvious, when he thought about it. If they had shadowed him, as he suspected they probably had, there was not only the similarity in their appearance to confuse the watchers but also the similarity in their movements. They had travelled at the same time by the same means to and from Paris, and while there had done similar things. It was very probable that, like him, George R. had visited the offices of the *Journal d'Agriculture Practique* and the French Ministry of Agriculture to learn more about the current situation regarding phylloxera.

But would not murdering a Scotland Yard detective be thought a too dangerously provocative thing to do, bearing in mind fears of backlash against the Irish in Ireland and on the mainland? Or, then again, maybe they had become so extreme that they thought that such daring acts were necessary to frighten the government into submission or propel the Irish into all-out rebellion?

Helen would have none of this mistaken-identity theory. 'I think this whole business is getting you down,' she said, handing him a portion of treacle pudding. 'You need a rest from it.'

'What I *need* is more evidence. It's all dried up,' he complained, taking up his spoon and digging it into the sweet lemony mixture. 'But in any case I can't think of any other explanation of why George died. The Fenians haven't claimed responsibility and the ferociousness of the act seems to discount mere robbery.'

Helen was still unconvinced and explained why as he finished his pudding. 'Didn't you tell me that he had seemed nervous – or at least expectant – while on the ferry and that he made it clear he didn't want your company on the train?'

Best laughed. 'I wouldn't put it as bluntly

as that. At least *he* didn't.'

Helen laughed too. 'I realize no one in his right senses would choose *not* to have your company. But it does suggest that he had some other kind of arrangement in hand. If, as you said, he was a sociable man and you got on so well, I can't see any other reason.'

'He might have wanted to go to sleep. Or to read some important papers. You know what it's like. Even sociable people need a rest from company sometimes.'

'Hmm,' said Helen. She paused, frowned, then said, 'If I were you I should look more to this phylloxera business.'

'That's what Cheadle said.'

'Well, you know he's always right.'

They both raised their eyes heavenward and laughed, then, obviously with the intention of steering him onto lighter subjects, Helen asked whether he had heard any more from the oh-so-calm Miss Bennett.

He shook his head. 'Not a word.'

'So that means her brother has *not* returned?'

'Seems so. But I wouldn't bank on it. People are quick to call on us when they are in trouble but slow to let us know when the trouble has abated.'

He felt guilty about not telling her that he had left a letter for collection by G.C., but he knew she would only worry. Instead, he said,

190

'I can't understand why anyone is taken in by these newspaper pleas and offers,' and went on to amuse her by describing one advertiser who guaranteed to reveal the means of making a fortune without risk or outlay – on receipt of a small sum of money.

'And people sent him money?' said Helen, eyes wide.

'Oh yes,' he laughed. 'They answered in droves. In return they received a slip of paper saying, "Waste not, want not. Save every penny and waste not a moment." '

'I don't believe it. Did you catch him?'

He nodded. 'But for another swindle, later on. There were no complaints about that one at the time because people were afraid of looking foolish.'

'As well they might be!' She furrowed her brow. 'So, what did you charge him with?

Best shrugged. 'We didn't. It was a little tricky. He claimed he was quite sincere.' He laughed. 'In any case, the second swindle was much more serious, to do with mortgage securities, and he received sufficient punishment on that.'

So many French people lived in Soho that when there (observed the Scottish topographer William Maitland in 1740) it was an easy matter for a stranger to imagine himself in France. These residents were largely descendants of the Huguenots, French Protestants who had escaped persecution by Louis XIV. Later, they were joined by French refugees of a different stripe, those fleeing the French Revolution, its aftermath and later political eruptions.

By the time Best arrived in Soho on that frosty morning in January 1884, overcrowded and raffish Soho was no longer quite so exclusively French. Now there were also many Germans and Italians, plus a generous sprinkling of various other nationalities. But the French atmosphere still dominated and was evident in the ownership of the small cafés, restaurants, hotels, pubs, shops and brothels.

Best and his colleagues were well acquainted with many of Soho's more dubious establishments, being frequently called upon to visit them at the behest of the French police in search of swindlers, thieves and murderers who had fled across the Channel. He now spent a wearying day combing through them in search of the two railway passengers whom Mr Coates had assisted. Had there not been this Fenian problem he might have called upon Smith and various other colleagues to lend a hand but Williamson had made it clear that none could be spared.

He also made contact with a police informer who hung about in a seedy Dean

Street pub. He swore he had heard nothing of two French peasants hiding from the police.

He ended this frustrating day sitting at a table in the bar of the Hotel Bordeaux just off Leicester Square absorbing the potent aromas of French tobacco and coffee while awaiting the arrival of the owner who had slipped out 'to meet someone'. It was at this hotel that his Yard colleague, Detective Inspector Moser, had recently found a man whom the Belgian police were seeking for decamping with a cache of diamonds that did not belong to him.

The hotel proprietor, the lugubrious, balding, bespectacled Jacques Bouschet, knew that the police could close him down any time for harbouring criminals. He also knew that they were more than happy to allow him to remain open, their job being made infinitely easier when they knew where they might lay their hands on their prey. But an element of compromise was necessary on both sides. While not enquiring too assiduously about lesser criminal fry (which would give the place a bad reputation among the local low life and frighten them away) the detectives expected cooperation when it came to more serious matters.

When M. Bouschet finally arrived, Best made it plain that this was indeed a serious matter before enquiring whether he had seen the two men. There was little reaction as he began describing them.

'Could be anyone,' Bouschet said with a shrug.

But when Best mentioned the mole on the cheek of one of them the man's stillness answered for him as did the twitching of his mouth when it came to the pipe with a bowl shaped like the head of Queen Victoria. As Best had anticipated, the sight of the head of the great and glorious Queen Empress being grasped in the gnarled and none-too-clean fist of a French peasant had amused the hotelier and did so again in retrospect.

Best now had his answer and was not prepared to tiptoe around the subject any further. He reiterated that this was a very serious business then went straight to the heart of the matter by asking bluntly, 'Are they here now?'

The man's mouth tightened. He lowered his head and fixed his eyes on the glass inkstand that lay on the reception-desk counter. Eventually, he looked up at Best over his half spectacles and shook his head.

Best bypassed more questions by commanding, 'Show me their room.'

Bouschet gazed at him thoughtfully for a moment, tap, tap, tapping on the counter with his right middle finger as he did so.

Then, after glancing around to check whether anyone was watching, he turned towards the green-baize board on the wall behind him and lifted off the key to room seventeen.

As Best took it from him he was all too aware that he would be no match for two sturdy Frenchmen with nothing to lose should they return while he was in their room. 'Find me a policeman,' he commanded.

This was too much for the landlord. His eyes became angry and he opened his mouth to object. Best stayed him with an upraised hand and pointed out that injury to a Scotland Yard detective on his premises due to his refusal to assist him would bring down such wrath that neither he nor his establishment would survive.

'After I've gone you may inform your friends that I came in here and seized the key before you could stop me. You sent for a constable to protect yourself because you thought I was a blackguard intent on robbery. There's a lot of it going on at the moment, even,' he said looking round pointedly, 'in the best hotels.'

Dazed by this barrage of threats and instructions, Bouschet stood transfixed for a moment until Best snapped out, 'Get a constable *now*. Let him in the back way and send him upstairs to me. If I find that you have warned these men away I will charge you with obstructing the police in the execution of their duty and have this hotel closed down!'

Twenty-Three

To say that room seventeen was small would be an understatement. To get alongside the bed one had first to close the door, and two people could not pass each other without one of them pinning themselves against the wall.

The room's dark brown paintwork was peeling and there were damp patches on the walls while the musty smell of the bedding mingled unpleasantly with the pungent aroma of coarse pipe tobacco. Soho's only select hotels were in and around Leicester Square but the Bordeaux was not one of them.

The tiny wardrobe, which stood alongside the window that looked out onto a brick well, was empty. As was the drawer in the small, rickety bedside table.

'They have no belongings?' Best raised his eyebrows.

Bouschet nodded.

Customers who arrived without luggage were not usually popular with hoteliers due to their tendency to depart quietly without paying the bill.

'They paid in advance.'

Ah. With money from George R.'s wallet, perhaps.

'How long for?'

'Five nights.'

Now why did they do that? In fact, if their only quarrel was with George R., why hadn't they just turned around and gone straight back over the Channel? Were they waiting for something? Payment from the Fenians?

'What are they like?'

'Peasants.'

He didn't exactly spit out the word but it was said with all the disdain of a metropolitan animal who felt himself much more worldly wise than those who spent their time tilling the soil.

'Small farmers, maybe?'

He shrugged. 'Maybe. I don't know.'

'Where were they from?'

'The North? The Loire, somewhere like that.'

Best was lifting up the pillows to see what

might be hidden under them. 'What are they doing here?'

For Bouschet this was obviously one question too many. This time his arms went up to accompany the shrug. 'How should I know?'

'You must have some idea. They're not your usual sort of customers.'

'Why should I? Why should I? People come and go. If I asked them all why – I would have no customers. It is their business what they are doing here.'

'And sometimes ours,' warned Best as he began lifting the mattress to feel about underneath, 'if they are criminals.'

Bouschet did not answer. He was still resentful about being obliged to invite a uniformed police constable into his establishment. The PC was now secreted behind a door in the corridor ready to come to Best's aid.

Best's hand had just fastened onto a hard, knobbly object tucked well towards the centre of the mattress when he heard footsteps coming along the corridor. Bouschet's head went up. He had heard them too.

Best held up his right forefinger and hissed, 'Not a sound or you will regret it bitterly.'

They both stood immobile as the door opened quietly and a man shuffled in, head down, preoccupied. He stopped suddenly as he glimpsed their shoes and trousers; a puzzled expression came onto to his face to be replaced by shock and then realization. As he turned to flee Best grabbed his arm, banging the door closed with the other hand and shouting for the PC, who came pounding along the corridor in his heavy boots.

By the time he got there the struggle was almost over. The suspect had suddenly gone limp and sat down on the bed, where he began to cry.

The officers of Vine Street reckoned that their police station was at the hub of the universe: Piccadilly Circus. How could it be otherwise, situated right in the heart of London, the capital of the greatest empire the world had ever known?

Oddly, however, while famous, the station was at the same time secret, hidden from view. Unless you knew where it was, in a narrow little street at the end of a narrower little street off Piccadilly, you would never find it.

The station's appearance, too, was remarkably unimpressive, particularly considering it was the divisional headquarters. A plain flat-fronted four-storey brick building, flanked by two public houses, one next door and one at the end of the little street. Even some of the smaller inconsequential suburban stations had steps leading up to arched entrances surmounted by the force's crest and so had more dignity and gravitas than Vine Street. Here, there was just a plain doorway opening straight out onto the street. Only the small blue lamp jutting from its walls and the heavily barred ground-floor windows revealed its function. Like Scotland Yard, thought Best, it does not live up to its fame.

Vine Street's catchment area was one of extreme contrasts, including as it did parts of prosperous and elegant Mayfair, the raffish and poverty-stricken Soho and the gentleman's clubland of St James's. Superintendent Dunlap, the man in charge of C Division, had two major obsessions: the comfort of his men, whom he complained were poorly housed, and concern over the rapidly increasing number of pubs, restaurants and theatres in this, at less than a mile square, the smallest division of Metropolitan Police. These places of entertainment were attracting larger and larger crowds of people, he complained, many of them of 'a troublesome class', as well as encouraging the great nuisance of prostitution.

It was to this unique police station that Best took his prisoner after insisting that

Bouschet identify the man then summon them a cab.

Bouschet had been right. Faucon did look like a peasant or at least a simple man who spent his time outdoors in hard labour and had neither the time nor the inclination to bother about his appearance. He was short and stocky in stature; constant physical labour had made his shoulders broad and hard and his hands calloused and scarred. His complexion was reddened and roughened by constant exposure to the elements and his wayward eyebrows and sprouting nose and ear hairs had been left to go their own way. His clothes were crumpled and his chin had three days' dark growth.

The contrast between him and the immaculate Best could not have been more striking but Best found the man's simplicity refreshing. Unfortunately, whenever the detective inspector tried to question this hardy man of the soil he burst into tears. It was a pathetic sight but Best reminded himself that he was almost certainly one of the men who had so cruelly disposed of George R. The tears, as with those of most villains, were doubtless for himself and the fact that he had been caught.

Weary of getting no sense from him, Best got permission to leave him in a cell until he had quietened down then went off to find himself a cup of tea. To give a suspect time to recover from the shock of arrest was not usually a good idea, but there was little else he could do.

He took his tea into the library reading room used by the single men who lived in bleak dormitories in the nearby section house. Such rooms were a recent innovation at police stations and they delighted Superintendent Dunlap as they not only offered some comfort around a fireplace but also helped stop the men seeking it in the nearby pubs.

Vine Street's library and reading room was particularly cheerful, being hung about with engravings, maps and ornamental busts. The introduction of a billiard table had increased its popularity. Even married men came in early for a game, reported Superintendent Dunlap, or stayed after duty to play.

Best went there not only because it was warmer and more cheerful than the station's back office but because he wanted to talk to some of the men. He knew that his chances of a rapid arrest of the second Frenchman, Georges Maillet, were small. The word would have raced around Soho, reaching even the most recent strangers and fugitives. The station sergeant had agreed to tell his men to look out for Maillet, but this would be only one of a dozen instructions and informations issued to them when they paraded for duty. Much better to make direct contact with the men, particularly with those who wanted to become detectives.

Those who already were detectives, divisional detectives that is, would have to be placated. Not only did they resent the Yard detectives and the publicity they received but they imagined themselves looked down upon by them and they might not be pleased that the owner of the Hotel Bordeaux had been antagonized either.

On the other hand, Best *was* a Scotland Yard detective inspector of long standing and some fame and experience. His good opinion might just help them to be selected to come to the Yard, as it had John George Smith nine years earlier.

Best had been so impressed by John George's quickness and enthusiasm when he gave him divisional assistance during a murder enquiry related to the Regent's Park Explosion that he had insisted he stay on the case. He was pleased now to see that one of the better divisional detectives, young Detective Constable Hills, was in the reading room, where he was engrossed in a French-language textbook. He clearly had his sights set on the Yard.

The lanky lad was excited to see Best and

get a chance to talk to him but was trying hard not to make it obvious to his colleagues. In turn, Best took care not to appear too familiar with him, even though he had known his father quite well, as he had Smith's. He was happy to pass on his request to someone who would take notice and not obstruct him deliberately out of spite.

Back in the cells he found Faucon fast asleep. A not unusual reaction. Being on the run could be exhausting as could a desperate resisted arrest and the humiliation of being handcuffed for a journey to a strange police station. Sometimes, the sheer relief of being caught, no longer having to run and hide and look over your shoulder all the time made prisoners relax – and fall asleep.

At least, thought Best, while he was asleep Faucon couldn't cook up an alibi. But doubtless, he and his accomplice had done that already. However, the problem with a shared tale was that one person usually got some small detail wrong or omitted an important element, and that could be used to catch them out.

The recently awakened are usually at their most vulnerable, not having had time to gather their thoughts. Therefore, once Best had roused his prisoner he immediately asked whether he and his friend Maillet had travelled on the Continental express from Dover to London on the afternoon in question.

'Yes,' Faucon replied.

'Was there another man in your compartment?'

'Yes,' said Faucon.

Best almost frowned. Was it really going to be this easy? Sometimes it was. His French was good enough for him not to require an interpreter but he was beginning to wonder whether he was understanding the man correctly. He decided to stop leading up to the important questions.

'Tell me what happened,' he said.

Faucon stared at him for a moment, his sleep-creased eyes wide. Then he opened his mouth. No sound came out. He tried again. This time it did and he told Best exactly what had happened.

Twenty-Four

'This is about phylloxera?'

'Of course! Of course! It was all his fault in the first place!' exclaimed Faucon. 'Then, when we find a way to put it right, he is only interested in the important growers – ' he spread his arms wide and spat out in disgust – *'les gros-bonnets*. He refuses to help us unless we pay him huge amounts of money for his vine roots.'

Best found it hard to believe that the Southern gentleman he had met would behave in such a way but, as he knew, people were not always what they seemed to be. Also, he reminded himself, this was only Faucon's side of the story.

'We told him, we told him...' It was spilling out uncontrolled.

Best stopped him. 'Just a minute. I want to know the whole story. In what way was it *his* fault in the first place?'

'All the Americans and yours as well,' he

insisted. 'You brought in infected vines and...'

Best waved his hand rapidly to get the man's attention. 'Stop! Stop! I don't want to know about everyone's. Just *his*.'

He was aware that the French blamed the English as well as the Americans for the importation of phylloxera. It was true, the disease had first been noticed on American vines in an English greenhouse. But the French themselves had imported masses of American vines when they were fighting an attack of the vine mould oïdium.

'Infected vines came from his nursery in Missouri!'

Best seemed to remember that George R. had said he came from Georgia. George from Georgia, he had thought, but he let that pass.

'At first it was just in the Midi. We thought we were safe. It was a long way away and there was much talk of a cure, a solution. Always much talk. The sulphurists kept claiming that their method was working but all the time this creature was creeping towards us. Then,' he put his hands to his head despairingly, 'it reached the Loire.'

Best reached out and patted his arm. 'It must have been terrible.'

Faucon shook his head. 'We had no grand chateau. *We* had never made a *grand cru*. We were just hardworking small farmers guarding our vines from frost at night and mould and weeds and insects by day. Then taking our grapes to the winery and selling them for enough to feed our families and buy a few indulgences,' he said sadly. 'We had struggled when the oidium struck but eventually all was going well again. Then came this terrible louse.

'That man made a fortune selling the vines to France then, when we were in trouble, he wanted to make more, always more. Even if we could pay his prices and do the grafting and planting we would not get a crop that year and we would have to wait for three more years for the new vines to grow. We wrote to him and begged him but it was no good ... He said no, and we were finished.'

Best was perplexed. 'So you decided to *kill* him?'

'No! No!' shouted Faucon. 'That was never our intention!'

'Tell me what was. What you were doing on that train?'

'We had decided to make one last effort. The other small growers banded together to pay our expenses. We were to try to make some sort of arrangement with him. We tried to speak to him in Paris but could not get him alone. We had to get him alone to explain our situation, and maybe touch his heart. But we couldn't. So we followed him, waiting for our opportunity. We had no chance on the ferry either but on the train at last we got him alone. But then he tried to kill us!'

'What?' exclaimed Best. '*He* tried to kill *you*?' This story was becoming stranger and stranger.

Faucon nodded. 'He took out a knife and tried to kill us.'

'But why? You must have threatened him?'

'No! No!' Faucon became even more agitated, waving his hands in the air in an effort to brush away the very notion. 'He denied everything. He said that what we were saying was all lies. He kept telling us to buy American vines and go to school. It was an insult. Then he took out a knife and kept pushing it at us.' He paused then said, 'We had no choice but to take ours out and defend ourselves.' He looked away. 'By then we were so angry and tired...' He spread his hands. There was a long silence before he whispered, 'We didn't mean to kill him. But he fought us. Called us thieves!'

Best lowered his head into his hands. He could see exactly what had happened. George R. had shown *him* the knife when describing the grafting technique. It was a big knife with a straight three-inch blade and a long wooden handle and a small spatula on the end with which to open up the grafts. He'd claimed it was the latest American design and pointed out that the blade had to be straight; curved ones were no good, neither were the pruning knives that some people tried to use. There were machines that could make the cut now, he'd said, but small growers still needed to be taught how to graft with a knife. And they were eager, he said. He had described grafting lessons, held in a town hall in the Midi, which had been overwhelmed by farmers wanting to learn. He had also told Best that his poor command of French hampered him when trying to teach the method. Was that what had cost him his life? His poor French?

Best could picture it all too clearly. George R. had taken out his knife; they had misunderstood his intentions and drawn theirs. Believing they wanted to rob and kill him he had thrust out. They lost control and attacked him with a frenzy born of long-held anger, hate and frustration. What Best still couldn't understand or believe was this picture he was painting of the friendly and generous American he had met. Faucon had called him *méchant* – wicked – and described him as hard-hearted and mercenary. It all seemed so at odds with the man's declared intentions.

There was no doubt about one thing,

though. They had killed George R. Hardinge and it was now up to the courts to decide their fate.

He escorted Faucon through to the charge room feeling no elation at having solved the crime, merely an overwhelming sadness about the tragedy of it all.

The station sergeant sat behind the large charge-room desk while Faucon stood opposite and Best alongside. He gave the brief facts of the case and explained why he had suspected Faucon and his colleague, repeating each sentence in French as he went. Finally he said: 'I told him I was arresting him on suspicion of murdering Mr George Ronald Hardinge.'

The drooping figure of Faucon suddenly sprang upright.

'No!' he cried. 'No! I did not kill this man. Only Barton! Only Barton! Who is this Hardinge!'

'It really was a case of mistaken identity after all,' Best said to Helen when he described his most embarrassing moment as a police officer. 'But George R. wasn't mistaken for me but for another American vine-nursery owner who really was profiteering from their misfortune.' He shook his head. 'I should have realized when he said his vine nursery was in Missouri. I thought it was in Georgia

211

and I was right.'

'But how could they make such a mistake? It's unbelievable.'

'It was a chapter of misunderstandings. They had not met the real man, Edgar Barton Junior, only corresponded with him. He wouldn't agree to a meeting so they went to Paris to find him.'

Best rolled over in bed and propped his head up on his hand. 'They heard he was at the American Club but they weren't allowed in the bar so they bribed the waiter to let them look in and he pointed out this Edgar Barton to them. Either he pointed out the wrong man or they mistook what he said.'

Helen sighed. 'Tragic.'

'They waited outside and tried to stop George on the street but he thought they were beggars or robbers and shooed them away so they determined to follow him until they could talk to him when he was alone.'

'But to follow him all the way to *England*?'

'They were desperate and others were depending on them.'

'Two more questions, then you can go to sleep.'

Now she had him thoroughly awakened he had other plans but he nodded. 'Yes?'

'Why didn't they go straight back to France? They could have escaped.'

'They were waiting for things to die down. They didn't know that the body was lying undiscovered in a field. They thought it was by the track and would be found straight away and then we would be watching the ports for them. But all we were looking for was more Fenians. And the second question?' he said moving towards her in what she termed his predatory manner.

'Why did George R. seem to be expecting someone?'

'I've no idea, yet. But...'

'I think I know the answer. He knew he was being followed and was anxious about it.'

'That is a possibility I am considering. But you have asked your two questions, therefore I claim my reward.'

Scotland Yard detectives were renowned for acting with dispatch only when there was a reward in view.

'You haven't closed the case yet,' she laughed. 'But I'll see if I can let you have something on account.' She paused. 'Just one more thing?'

'Yes,' he sighed into her hair.

'Do you believe him?'

Best stopped his nuzzling, 'What d'you mean? Yes, of course!'

'Hmm,' she said in that infuriating I-don't-agree-but-won't-argue manner. 'And why were they carrying such large knives?'

He sat up. There'd be no sleep now.

'I might as well go to bed with Cheadle!' he exclaimed.

Twenty-Five

The hunt was on for the second man: Georges Maillet. The ports had been warned and Best had managed to acquire the services of Detective Sergeant John George Smith. He sent him to Soho to exercise his more youthful charms on some of the barmaids and domestics.

Meanwhile, Best attended Bow Street Magistrates' Court with his dispirited prisoner. The case had been transferred there as the accused was a foreigner, and the Yard had taken over the case.

The court's two stipendiary magistrates were dubbed the Lion and the Lamb. Mr Vaughan, the lion, was tough and rigorous while Mr Field, the lamb, was soft-hearted, some thought to a ridiculous degree. He was given to making little exclamations of horror whenever a man's wickedness was revealed then turning around and telling hardened old defendants, 'Now let's hear your side of the story.' But he was kind to policemen too for which they were sometimes grateful.

But Best was pleased to see that they were on the Lion's list today. He was tired after a fairly sleepless night and wanted a quick response devoid of tutting and time-wasting searches for the better side of the defendant's nature. When Best asked for a week's remand in the hope of producing a fellow defendant for Faucon, Mr Vaughan responded with a few piercing questions then granted it with a sharp bang of his gavel.

Best seized the opportunity to spend more time with Faucon while he awaited the prisoner's van which would take him off to Holloway Prison.

The Frenchman's story never wavered although it had begun to feel even stranger to Best, possibly because Helen had found it so unconvincing. But she had not seen Faucon's genuine distress when he had confessed.

Then again, that could be *why* she might be right. Wasn't he always telling young detectives to ignore outward appearances of respectability, beauty and charm and to discount any demonstrations of honesty or remorse? Ignore their tears and separate the story from its tellers, he always said. Just close your eyes and listen to the facts. Let them speak to you. That so many criminals might have out-acted Henry Irving had been a lesson hard in the learning for Best himself.

On the other hand – and it was one of Best's good points and curses that he could always see both sides (an unusual trait in a man, Helen had informed him) – he also knew that circumstances altered choices. Wealthy people had no need to steal food. Desperate circumstances led to desperate acts and there was no doubt many of these French vine growers were desperate.

M. de Marcellin, the sympathetic official at the French Ministry of Agriculture, had informed him that some vignerons had committed suicide. He had felt very strongly that the government should help them buy the American vines just as they had assisted them with the sulphur spraying.

What I must do, and quickly, Best thought, is find the second man, Maillet. Then I will discover the whole truth. Either Faucon's story would be proven or it would be demolished as a lie. If Smith was unsuccessful today, tomorrow he would beg for several men to search Soho from top to bottom.

As it was, Smith had no luck. No one had seen Maillet. The man might be a stranger but he was French and, it seemed, the community was looking after its own. In some respects this was a little strange. Soho inhabitants were usually wary of drawing the amount of police attention that a thorough search for a murderer might bring.

The respectably dressed gentleman was loaded down with an assortment of baggage as he arrived at the luggage repository of the London, Brighton and South Coast Railway in Victoria Station on the evening of Monday 25 February 1884.

He had a large canvas portmanteau of a foreign make, a small Gladstone bag and two boxes. One of the boxes was especially heavy and he asked Thomas, the cloakroom porter, to handle it with great care. In fact, so particular was he that when Thomas stacked the rest of the luggage on top of the box he said, 'Don't do that, please,' and asked him to place all of the bags and boxes on the floor, side by side, close together but with nothing on top of them.

Thomas obliged. The request was a little strange but then passengers often were, the porter had discovered, particularly when they were tired after a long journey. It was as well to placate them. Perhaps the man had travelled from Dieppe via Newhaven and had brought with him some delicate French porcelain and other souvenirs that he wanted to protect? Possibly even a clock, he could certainly hear one ticking but that was not unusual. Passengers often put travel clocks in their luggage.

Thomas had little time to contemplate the matter further, soon being distracted by two sailors, bound for Liverpool the following day, who came in to deposit their kitbags overnight. He was short of space so he ignored instructions of the fussy passenger and placed these on top of his boxes, portmanteau and Gladstone bag. It would all be gone by the time he returned the following day. As more luggage came in it, too, joined the pile on the floor. At midnight the depository closed and Thomas went home. It had been a long and busy day.

By one o'clock in the morning the last of the passengers had been decanted from the final trains and a feeling of peace and tranquillity was spreading over the darkening terminal.

Mr Manning, the night-duty inspector, was now in charge. He and his men were locking the doors, turning off gas jets and attaching the fire hose to the hydrant on one of the platforms, a nightly procedure that readied them for any unexpected outbreaks of fire which, although they might also occur during the day, were not so likely to go unnoticed then.

Suddenly the tranquillity was abruptly shattered by a deafening roar. Two of the men on the platform turned around in time to see the tail end of a red flash and flying debris coming from the luggage repository in the entrance hall. Two more were closer and were injured by the blast.

Almost instantly the glass and slate roof of the nearby booking office crashed to the ground and the walls of the cloakroom, booking office, first-class waiting room and inspector's office caved in. An eerie silence followed and at first the men were too stunned to react, then were hesitant in case more explosions should follow.

The entrance hall was now covered in rubble, glass, the fallen wooden roof, railway tickets and damaged luggage and the air full of choking dust. Flames quickly began to lick around the wrecked buildings.

Mr Manning rallied his men. They rushed to help the injured and lengthened the fortuitously coupled fire hose and dragged it towards the fire which, fed by fractured gas mains, was steadily gaining strength.

The explosion had been heard by the Victoria Street Fire Brigade and their engines soon arrived to add their considerable water-power to help quench the blaze.

Police Superintendent Hambling of B Division was also quick to arrive on the scene. He placed a police cordon around the site and asked that the wreckage not be interfered with in any way until it was examined by expert eyes. Telegrams were sent off to Superintendent Williamson, Colonel Majendie, Her Majesty's Chief Inspector of Explosives, and his assistant, Colonel Ford. When they arrived, the colonels brought with them their powerful magnet with which they began to comb through the wreckage.

Quite quickly these experts came to the conclusion that from the pattern of the damage and the discovery among the debris of the remnants of a small metal box and a metal spring, the explosion had *not* been caused accidentally by an accumulation of steam or gas. Nor was gunpowder the culprit because a large amount would have been necessary to cause such widespread damage. Therefore, the fiendish device must have been loaded with dynamite. From then on, the incident was referred to by the newspapers as the Dynamite Outrage.

As they surveyed the glass-and-ticket-strewn debris it also occurred to them, as *The Times* was later to comment, that perhaps it was fortunate that the buildings were not of a very imposing or substantial character. Indeed, as the newspaper added sarcastically, the station was constructed 'much after the fashion in vogue among people who live in constant apprehension of earthquakes'.

They went on to point out that had the offices been on the ground floor of lofty buildings, as was the case at many important railway stations, the consequences might have been much more serious. Reading this, Best felt that the railway companies concerned might easily take comfort from these words and feel justified in maintaining the ramshackle straggle of buildings that made up Victoria Station.

All that aside, what really concerned Williamson, Littlechild and Vincent was, were there more bombs out there? The Fenians had developed a habit of setting off several bombs at once so as to terrify the maximum number of people. If that was the case here, where were the rest of the fiendish devices? In trains? On omnibuses or cabs? Beside government offices? Under public monuments, or, God forbid, in the Houses of Parliament or at Buckingham Palace? It didn't bear thinking about.

When Best reported for duty the following morning he soon realized that the chances of his acquiring extra men to search Soho for Maillet were non-existent. Instead, detectives were issued with the description of the man who had handed in the suspect luggage the previous evening and told to look for him in places frequented by the Irish. The description was surprisingly full given that Mason, the porter, had only seen the passenger for a short time. The fact that he had made a fuss about the placement of his luggage had doubtless impressed the man's image on his mind.

He was, they were informed, twenty-nine years of age (which Best found an oddly precise figure), 5ft 10in to 5ft 11in in height (again, oddly precise), square built, with a large round face, light brown hair and a slight moustache; he turned his toes out when walking, had a soldierly appearance and wore a light tweed 'tourist suit'.

This description clearly pleased Cheadle, who was always chiding the CID about their scanty depictions of suspects. If a busy cloakroom porter could provide them with this, well ... He was, of course, particularly pleased about the walk. A person's walk and carriage were two of Cheadle's pet obsessions.

How could they miss him with all that information? The answer, of course, was quite easily. He would probably be back on the Continent by now having had time to catch the night express to Calais via Dover.

'I'll take Soho,' said Best.

'Me, too,' said Smith.

Cheadle seemed about to object and send them instead to Whitechapel, Deptford or Camden Town.

'I'm still not certain that Faucon was not involved with the Fenians,' Best explained. 'So I need to catch the second man. This way I can look for both: the square-built man with turned-out toes and Maillet. When I get Maillet I may be able to get information out of him about the bombs.'

'Oh, all right,' sighed Cheadle, not fooled nor missing the tongue-in-cheek element of Best's remark but choosing not to comment. He *had* mellowed. 'But only you. Smith is going down to Deptford.'

The Victoria Station bomb had exploded in the early hours of Tuesday 26 February 1884. The following evening the cloakroom porter at Charing Cross Station was searching, as instructed, for items of luggage of a suspicious character, particularly those that seemed more than ordinarily heavy.

He found a black portmanteau of 'a common material', which had been left by an American gentleman on Monday 25 February between the hours of seven and nine in the evening. The bag was fastened with two leather straps but not locked and was in fact extraordinarily heavy. He put it to one side for examination.

When opened it was found to contain a few items of old clothing, and below them, packed around a small tin box, many slabs of some heavy, solid material wrapped in paraffin-waxed paper. Each slab bore the words Atlas Powder 'A'. The police were called and they took the portmanteau to Woolwich Arsenal, in a cab.

This unexploded bomb, for that is what it proved to be, provided Colonel Majendie with a great deal of information. He already knew that Atlas Powder 'A' was in fact a form of lignine dynamite manufactured in the United States for industrial purposes but not legally imported into Britain. Inside the tin box was an American alarm clock of 'Peep of the Day' design. The back had been removed and a small nickel-plated waistcoat-pocket pistol fastened to the movement by copper wire. When the alarm went off at midnight one end of the handle would strike the trigger and fire the pistol into the detonator. The procedure had worked perfectly. The alarm had gone off, the trigger had been struck and the gun had fired – but the detonating cartridge had failed to ignite. The clock itself had wound down and finally stopped at 4.14 a.m.

The clock found in a suspect portmanteau at Paddington Station was still ticking merrily away. In this instance, a small knob had caught against the mechanism and prevented it from firing. Any doubt as to the source of this lethal package was dispelled when a recent copy of the *New York Sun* was found among the extra padding.

The duties of the porter at Ludgate Hill Station were heavy for, as *The Times* was later to remark, this railway (the London, Chatham and Dover) did not have a superabundance of station help. He, too, had been ordered to look out for suspect luggage and had even been told the approximate weight to expect. But really he had just not had time to do so. Indeed, the instruction had quite slipped his mind until a passenger had remarked jovially that he hoped there was no dynamite in *their* luggage repository given that it was so near to the stairs which were used daily by thousands of passengers.

Therefore it was not until early Saturday morning that yet another portmanteau containing yet another infernal machine was located. The guilty porter duly informed Mr Bowman, the station master of Ludgate Hill and Holborn Viaduct stations, who called in the City of London Police.

They took charge of the portmanteau but brought Colonel Majendie to the bomb rather than the other way around. Again, the detonator had failed to explode. On testing all of the detonators Majendie found that some of the cartridges worked, some had to be struck in a certain spot and others failed completely.

Now the Metropolitan Police were seeking four suspects, two of them American. Their descriptions varied from the scant to the quite extensive. The best of these described a short thirty-year-old man with a full beard, small features, short neck and stiff build who wore a brown mixture suit, black fur cap and white neck muffler. Oddly, the two sparsest descriptions were of the Americans, whom Best imagined might have attracted more attention.

The authorities decided that it was time to enlist the help of the public. They put up large posters offering a staggering £2,000 reward, half paid by the Home Office and the rest by the four railway companies concerned, for information leading to the arrest and conviction of the persons who left the bombs.

It was admitted, however, that the Charing Cross culprit had had sufficient time to catch the SER night train to Newhaven; the Paddington bomber could have departed immediately on the Great Western's express to Weymouth and thence by steamer to the Channel Islands or Cherbourg; and the Ludgate Hill Fenian had given himself time to take trains which could have deposited him safely in Flushing, Ostend or Calais long before the bombs had gone off or been found.

Meanwhile, serious questions were being asked in Parliament. Lord Randolph Churchill enquired of the Home Secretary whether he was considering legislation for expelling from the United Kingdom all foreign persons who might be reasonably expected by the police to have criminal designs against life or property by use of explosive agents.

He replied they already had some such powers but would apply for more should it be deemed necessary. Another Member of Parliament wondered why all luggage left at railway stations could not be searched.

The government were considering that as well.

Meanwhile, railway companies were refusing to accept bags weighing over 4lb *unless* the contents could be examined, and a *Times* correspondent suggested that all cloakroom porters should be issued with stethoscopes to detect ticking clocks inside the luggage.

Twenty-Six

On his way home after another fruitless search of Soho, Best went into a Notting Hill post office to enquire whether they had received a poste restante letter for Mr Conrad Lavoisier. They had.

Best had used a Germanic Christian name and a French surname as his nom de plume for his correspondence with G.C. to hamper any attempt to trace him and make enquiries about his financial position. When their attempts failed he hoped they would presume that he lived abroad and would stop trying.

G.C.'s reply was written on pale mauve paper. A clever touch, Best thought, hinting that in addition to her problems of the heart and pocket she had suffered a bereavement. However, lest a hot-blooded sympathetic male be put off by such an overwhelming catalogue of misery the paper also gave off a hint of lavender, although not so much as to suggest the extravagance of scented paper, which might indicate that G.C. had been rescued from penury.

I'm getting fanciful, thought Best. But as a sometime weaver of fantasies himself – in the line of duty, of course – he couldn't help admiring the clever touches in this one.

Alas, G.C. revealed in response to his most kind enquiry, her circumstances had not improved. In a graceful, flowery hand she declared herself most touched by his interest but admitted that she could not help feeling that life for her was over. She was at a loss to know where to turn next to survive, and though she realized it would be sinful to take the matter into her own hands, she was beginning to wonder whether that was the only course left open to her.

Strong meat. But this tragic tone must be getting results or they wouldn't be using it.

Nonetheless, G.C. rallied, she would be happy to meet him. Indeed, the very prospect provided the only faint glow of hope in her otherwise dimming world.

These romantic-fiction writers have much to answer for, thought Best.

If he would write and name a place or time, she went on, perhaps at some simple café where, if she could make so bold, he might buy her a bowl of soup (good heavens, Little Nell!), she would be there, waiting.

Ah, now there was the difficulty. The

authorities were panicking that more bombs were about to be planted, which led to more questions asking just what the police were doing about these threats.

Alarming reports were coming from Captain Robert Clipperton, the British Consul in Philadelphia, who ran a bevy of informants over there. Some time earlier he had warned them about a scheme to leave dynamite in handbags at sundry places with clockwork devices all set to explode at the same time. That had happened, as had attacks he had forecast in Liverpool.

Now he described Fenian plans to bomb all the London bridges at once and to get grenades into Parliament in books and bags and throw them onto the government benches from the Strangers' Gallery. Worse, two men were on their way over from the United States to explode a little dynamite near 'Her'. Not to harm Her but to get all the detectives in London guarding Her while they operated unhindered elsewhere.

Clipperton had also revealed the blood-curdling news that when someone had told O'Donovan Rossa that these actions could make the *English* rise against the Irish in their midst he said that that was exactly what they wanted to happen. Little wonder the Irish Republican Brotherhood were continuing to oppose the violence and consequently the Clan had broken off links with them.

The Home Office decided that drastic measures were needed to cope with these latest threats. Dublin Castle's spymaster, Edward Jenkinson, was brought over to London in secret and given a free hand. This Harrow-educated ex-Indian civil servant had been appointed the Irish Under Secretary for Police and Crime following the Phoenix Park murders. He held Robert Anderson in contempt but, like him, had formed a network of spies answerable only to himself and had been duly dubbed Spymaster General. He was equally unimpressed by Scotland Yard's Special Irish Branch, whose members he thought were unable to hold their tongues.

As a result of Clipperton's messages the Yard detectives were set to watch even more suspects. Best was given a prominent Fenian, Sheamus O'Mahoney, but hoped that once he knew the man's habits he might be reasonably certain of being able to make and keep an appointment with G.C. The trouble with many Fenians, particularly those in Paris, was that their lives were anything but regular. But O'Mahoney was a London-based family man so Best was hopeful.

He did not get an opportunity until, one wet Thursday afternoon, the man took a cab to St Pancras Station, where he boarded a train for Birmingham.

Best hurriedly sought out a Midland Railways policeman and asked him to telegraph the Birmingham City Police requesting they meet him on his arrival and the Yard to tell them where he had gone.

The engine was getting up steam and the carriage doors had all been closed when Best dragged one open again and jumped in, ticketless, with only seconds to spare. Fortunately, a quiet word with the ticket inspector en route not only saw him through but obliged him to resist the offer of a seat in first class – near O'Mahoney.

At Birmingham, he happily handed over his quarry and took the train back to London. There, he left one Gothic fantasy, St Pancras Station, and proceeded to another, Holloway Prison, where he asked to see Faucon.

The bombers' reward posters had given him an idea. The poster that had requested information about the murderer or murderers of George R. Hardinge had, as usual, offered a pardon to any accomplice, not being the actual murderer, who would give evidence that led to the capture and conviction of the guilty party.

The reaction to these offers of pardon could be startling. Criminals rushed to claim their presence at, but innocence of, the murder and sometimes in the process handed their pals over to the hangman. The justice thus obtained was dubious but, some felt, better than none at all.

Faucon's eyes had grown dead and his face was already exchanging its ruddy outdoor glow for a grey prison pallor. He had ceased crying and sunk instead into a hopeless despair. Best could hardly blame him. His outlook was bleak. He had committed murder, albeit through mistake and misunderstanding, but Best now doubted that a judge would see this as mitigating circumstance sufficient to save him from the gallows. Having had time to contemplate his deeds, the horror, remorse and waste of it all had sunk in and overwhelmed him.

Best knew he was not a monster, just a simple farmer led to act out of character by the awful situation in which he had found himself.

As the Frenchman had already confessed to the crime, Best could not offer him a pardon if he blamed it all on Maillet but, he explained, if he claimed that Maillet had struck the first blow and if he was absolutely honest with them about the reason for the murder they might be able to save him from the gallows and possibly even get his life sentence reduced.

Faucon refused utterly to blame his friend.

'It was both of us,' he insisted. 'We lost our minds – and,' he added sadly, 'our souls also.'

Best admired his loyalty and hoped that Maillet, if caught, would prove as loyal to him, but he persisted in probing for the real reasons for the murder.

Faucon knitted his brow and stared at him, puzzled. 'I do not know what you mean. What real reasons?'

'That you were paid to do it by the Fenians.'

Faucon was astonished. 'Paid!' he exclaimed. 'What are you talking about! We were not paid by anyone. We are not assassins!' The anger in his eyes showing how deeply he felt the insult.

'So,' Best persisted, 'you had no connection with the Fenians? It could help you if you—'

'Fenians? Who *are* these Fenians? Why should I kill for *them*?'

He stared at Best as though he were mad. There was a short silence eventually broken by Best, who explained, 'They are Irish-Americans who are trying to free Ireland from British rule.'

Faucon looked even more incredulous. 'What have they to do with *us*?'

'Nothing, it seems,' agreed Best, feeling rather foolish. He paused, pushed some pipe

234

tobacco over the table and persisted, 'So the reasons for the murder, mistaken though they were, are the ones you have already given me?'

'Of course! I confessed, didn't I? *Mon dieu*, what more do you want?'

'Nothing,' said Best. 'Nothing.'

Twenty-Seven

'It seems we were wrong about Faucon,' said Best.

'I was wrong,' Helen replied, 'it was me who had the doubts.'

Best shrugged. 'They were reasonable doubts, I suppose. Just as well to air them.' He paused. 'We seem to be exchanging characteristics. I'm too easily hoodwinked nowadays and you've become a doubter.'

She half-turned from her painting to look at him. 'But *you* were right.'

'Well, we think so. But we haven't caught Maillet yet. He may tell a different story.'

She changed her brush for a smaller one and picked up some creamy-white mix from her palette. 'Did he say why they were carrying the knives?'

'He claims they were for self-defence. That it's dangerous travelling on trains in France.'

'Well, they proved it's dangerous travelling on trains anywhere.' She turned back to her painting of foundling girls singing in their chapel and placed a highlight along a pleat in one of their strangely shaped caps. 'So where do you think Maillet is hiding?'

'The French police say he hasn't come home.'

'They would tell you if he had?' She wiped off the highlight, murmuring, 'Too much.'

'Well, we usually find *their* wanted men and they find ours.'

'Yes, usually, but there is a subtle difference this time.' She picked up more of the creamy mix.

He frowned. 'Oh, you mean it's usually French criminals escaping from them, whereas this is a French criminal escaping from *us*?'

She nodded, not speaking as she concentrated on applying a narrower strip of highlight, then stood back and murmured, 'That's better.'

'And of course, we're not dealing with the Sûreté this time.'

She smiled at him. 'With all their clever ideas about detection and identification!'

Best and his colleagues were sensitive

236

about being accused of lagging behind their Parisian counterparts. It wasn't so long since their whole department had been remodelled into the CID in the Sûreté's image. Now, the French were experimenting with a scheme to combat the difficult problem of identifying suspects correctly. This Bertillonage, or anthropometrics, involved measuring a prisoner's hands, feet, legs, fingers, arm span, length and breadth of head and so on as well as the usual noting down of scars and eye and hair colour – all on the grounds that no two human beings could possibly be identical in all these characteristics.

'No two humans could possibly take measurements the same way,' had been Best's reaction when he heard about the scheme.

'We have quite good relations with the police in Paris,' Best insisted. 'Moser says they are often very helpful when he is Fenian-watching over there. It's just that – you know what it's like with rural forces. They don't want to be unpopular with the people they've got to live alongside. It's bad enough trying to get some of our own forces to help us even when we have been called in, so...'

'The French are unlikely to want to hand over one of their own to the dastardly English.'

'Exactly.'

She stood well back to view her efforts,

shrugged, laid down her brush and gave him a warm kiss. He refrained from commenting on the picture knowing that only irritated her unless she asked his opinion or the work was finished, although he sometimes teased her by making silly comments.

'You think I should go over to France and see for myself?'

'I'd rather you didn't! What do *they* say?' *They* were Cheadle, Williamson and Vincent.

'All they care about at the moment is preventing the fiendish devices being spread around and keeping Jenkinson at bay. He's making a terrible nuisance of himself and not being in the least helpful. Makes you wonder whose side he's on.'

'His own,' she said dryly and paused. 'So, have you got another Fenian to follow?'

'Not yet. I've got to be ready to take over if O'Mahoney comes back. He's very alert and conscious that he might be followed. The only others available to shadow him look too much like policemen.'

'Rather than oily foreigners like you!'

He grinned and gave her a smack on the bottom. He still couldn't believe he could get away with doing that. That she would just smile.

'Will O'Mahoney be gone long, do you think?'

He shrugged. 'Don't know. They say he's

238

met up with Daly, a Fenian the Birmingham police have been watching for months. One of Jenkinson's informants told him the man was into something big.'

'I thought they *all* were!'

'This one even more so, it seems. Anyway, Jenkinson is on tenterhooks in case Daly realizes he's being followed or they arrest him too soon and the others are warned off.'

'Well, at least that gives you a little break! Time to breathe.'

It also gave him time to meet G.C. Indeed, he had posted a letter to her on his way home that very evening.

Best chose the Strand area for their meeting. It was close enough to Scotland Yard that even if his duties suddenly took him elsewhere he could leave a message at the rendezvous.

He was a little less certain about which rendezvous to choose. Like Fleet Street, the Strand was home to many publishers and small businesses, and innumerable public houses. The latter, he felt, would not have the right atmosphere nor give the correct impression. In any case, many were no place to take a lady. A hotel tea room might suit, but it could also hint that she might like to repay his generosity in one of the upstairs rooms. The Strand had a louche reputation.

While suitably respectable, a Temperance coffee or cocoa room would convey a stingy impression, thus encouraging the notion that Mr Conrad Lavoisier might not be worth cultivating as a mark. In her letter G.C. had asked to be taken to somewhere simple and, who knows, while acting out her part she might arrive in pauper's guise. But he thought not. Not if seduction was on the menu. Poor but pretty was his guess. The obvious answer, he decided, was Gatti's.

With its Italian waiters, French rolls and cosmopolitan customers, Gatti's Royal Adelaide Gallery Restaurant and Café had an excitingly foreign flavour while the food was reassuringly British and the prices reasonable, an inspired combination that had resulted in an almost continuous expansion into nearby premises.

Much of its charm was due to its handsomely decorated, galleried and mirrored interior, inherited from the days when it had been the Adelaide Gallery of Science. Best ambled through the restaurant's ground floor, past mostly middle-aged men enjoying their chops and potatoes washed down with bitter from pewter mugs or reading newspapers and drinking tea. Later, he knew, one end of the long room would be alive with Continental émigrés smoking, chatting, playing chess or dominoes and planning revolutions back home. Just now it was fairly quiet.

He climbed the stairs to the gallery, where young couples were partaking of their sixpenny teas while gazing down on the great room below, then headed for the room beyond where a choicer menu was available.

He was ten minutes early. He sat down at one of the marble-topped tables as far back and as close to the wall as possible so that he could see everyone who entered and take note of those already present. If this was as well-organized a swindle as he imagined someone might be here looking him over and judging how much they could take him for.

There was only one man on his own and he was almost oddly out of place. A seedy-looking fellow wearing a tight jacket who looked as if he would be more at home card-sharping on a racetrack or downstairs among the smokers and newspaper readers rather than up here toying with a toasted tea cake. He doubted whether he would be there to spy on him. These swindlers would not make such a clumsy mistake.

In his letter Best had described himself as having a touch of the Italian or Spaniard about him rather than the Frenchman his name suggested. This was due, he explained, to his Italian mother. Well, at least that was true. It was always best to keep as near to the truth as possible. You were less likely to make mistakes that way.

He had also told her that he would be wearing a crimson-embossed silk waistcoat and in his cravat would be a tie pin set with a large moonstone clasped in a silver hand which itself was sparked off by a small diamond. In his buttonhole would be a red carnation and on his head, a soft felt hat.

Helen called this ensemble his dago disguise, a word she had learned from an American friend. It amused her that it was so contrary to the principles of the art, which insisted you fade into the background. Best explained that not only did it make him look different from the detectives in disguise portrayed in *Punch* and *Fun* cartoons, bowler-hatted, square of shoulder and looking as if they were about to salute or parade for duty, but it also helped him behave in a more expansive manner as befitted a man of Latin temperament.

He knew what G.C. looked like, having glimpsed her that day at the accommodation address and followed her down busy Fleet Street to Craven Buildings. He recalled that Mary, as the pale young man had called her, was most comely, all ripeness and helpless femininity.

Unsurprisingly, Best was looking forward

to seeing her again, although it did suddenly occur to him that if any friend of theirs saw him in what looked like a tryst with such a delightful young woman Helen might fail to understand that it was only in the cause of duty. Particularly when, for once, he had not told her what he was doing. He had donned his dago disguise at the office so that she wouldn't find out and start to worry.

Mary was late. Their appointment had been for three o'clock and it was now twenty minutes past. If a lady was ten minutes late it could enhance the pleasurable expectation. When it got to twenty or thirty minutes the feelings turned to concern laced with more than a hint of irritation.

He took his eyes from the door to take out his watch to check it against the café clock. Out of the corner of his eye he saw someone come into the room and the head waiter advancing towards them. He glanced up, watch still in hand, to find it was not the dark and delicious Mary, only a fair young woman with an uncertain air.

His eyes went back to his watch. Three twenty-five! He sighed. This was turning out to be a terrible waste of precious police time. He should have been out searching for Maillet. He felt guilty for indulging his curiosity while they were so busy with more serious matters.

He suddenly became aware that someone was standing over him, clearing their throat. He looked up. It was the fair young woman.

'Scuse me,' she said. 'Are you Mr Lav – Lavuser?'

He stared at her, startled, then nodded. 'Indeed, yes. I am Mr Lavoisier.'

She was quite pretty close to: a triangular face with pale blue eyes, pink and white cheeks and an upturned nose.

'I'm ever so sorry I'm late,' she said. 'I got lost.'

The pale blue eyes were close to tears. He stood up saying, 'That's all right, m'dear. These streets can be confusing.' He pulled out a chair and helped her sit down. 'I had began to worry that you might have been waylaid,' he smiled. 'Perhaps it was thought-less of me to have you come to this area.'

'Oh, no. It was no trouble, no trouble,' she insisted. 'It's my fault.' She gave him a wan smile.

This encounter was not turning out how Best had expected.

'I thought you might like the set tea,' he said, handing her the menu.

She took it uncertainly and looked at it equally uncertainly.

She was clearly relieved when he said, 'Is that all right?'

'Oh, yes. Yes.'

'No soup, I'm afraid but the cakes should make up for that.'

She looked puzzled but just smiled and said, 'Thank you. Thank you very much.'

'Having something simple like that will give us a chance to talk.'

She nodded but said nothing.

'What's your name?'

'Mary.'

Now wasn't that a coincidence? Another Mary.

'You use the initials G.C. in your advertisement.'

'Oh, yes.' This was clearly a question she had been expecting. 'It stands for the pet name that Freddie gave me.' She blushed and looked embarrassed. 'Gorgeous Canary. I was wearing yellow when we first met.'

He smiled. 'Pet names are fun, aren't they, even if they sound silly to other people?'

As he had expected her clothes were pretty but a little shabby: faded black dress and coat, frayed lace at her cuffs and around her neck.

Once their order had been taken she looked around, caught him watching her and said quickly, 'This is a nice place.'

He nodded. 'I thought you might like it. Now,' he patted her hand in a fatherly manner, 'tell me how you are getting on. I've been worried about you.'

To his surprise she blushed again and looked upset but she took a deep breath and launched into a clearly rehearsed recital of her woes.

Twenty-Eight

Once she began, Mary moved quite smoothly through her tale. It was a simple one but showed a certain amount of originality. Certainly a change from 'the master had his wicked way with me then threw me out on the streets'.

She began by describing how she had been an innocent country girl living in an Essex village when she met Freddie, the dashing young man from London. On the promise of marriage and an exciting life in the big city he had persuaded her away from the bosom of her family. At first, all had been well, despite several difficulties that had prevented them from getting married, and Freddie proving not to be quite the man about town that she had imagined. In fact, he was an ostler who looked after the horses which pulled the vans for an East End furniture warehouse.

But they were happy even though she missed her family and was lonely in their one-room basement while he was at work. Then one day on his rounds up West he met another woman. She was a widow and older than him and, he said, nowhere near as pretty as her. But she had lots of money. He began coming home late, insisting that he was only doing odd jobs for the widow. She paid him well and gave him expensive presents. Then he began staying out all night and, finally, he didn't come home at all.

She'd been desperate, not knowing where to turn for food and rent.

'Why didn't you go back home?'

'They wouldn't have me.' She lowered her eyes in well-rehearsed remorse. 'I'd shamed them going off with a man, unmarried an' all.'

'So, how did you live?'

She shook her head and looked away. 'I sold the few little bits of jewellery I had. But just the same I nearly starved. Then I saw these advertisements in one of the newspapers Freddie left behind – he followed the horses. Some of them asked people to get in touch – and I thought if he knew how desperate I was without him he would come back. So I put in an advertisement myself.'

'It was very well written,' said Best, recalling how it implored for help 'in my deepest hour of trial' and the 'in memory of the happy past I entreat your aid'.

'The man at the newspaper helped me. Said I had to make sure it touched the heart.'

'It certainly did that. Mine, anyway.'

Sadly, she revealed, even this pathetic plea failed to bring Freddie back but it did bring in some money sent by kind gentlemen who were touched by her plight.

'That 'elped me pay the rent and buy a little food, just enough to keep me alive.' She wrung her hands.

At that moment the waiter took some of the drama out of the situation by busying with teacups and saucers, plates of sandwiches and scones and a cake-stand piled high with a tempting assortment of maids of honour and fruit tartlets.

Once they had filled their cups, taken a few sips of tea and a few bites of sandwich to start, Best prompted her, 'You were telling me about your situation.'

She nodded, wiped crumbs from her lips and said, 'Yes. Oh yes.'

'Gentlemen sent you money so you could pay the rent...'

'Yes,' she nodded again, uncertainly, like a small girl trying to remember her lines in the school nativity play, nervous in case she forgot them or missed some words out altogether.

Suddenly, she was back on track. 'That's right. That's right. But it didn't last long.' The sad look again. 'I've been trying to get a situation – in domestic service – but I 'aven't got no references and they don't like people who don't 'ave references.'

'So what are you doing now?'

'Well, that's just it!' she exclaimed suddenly. 'The landlord says he's going to throw me out!'

Ah, here it comes. She must find the rent or there will be nothing for it but a life of shame.

'He says I'm not respectable. That I'm giving the place a bad name, a woman on my own. But I'm not like that! I'm not! I've tried to keep away from doin' that – but now it looks like...' A tear started into her eyes as she became carried away by the tale of her own sad predicament.

Best said nothing.

She picked up her cup with a trembling hand, gulped down a few mouthfuls of tea, looked at him appealingly over the rim and whispered, 'Would you do me a favour?'

He hesitated. 'Depends what it is.'

'Come back and see him for me. Tell him you're my uncle. That you give me an allowance and so I'm not one of those ... those...'

Again, he was taken by surprise. He'd

expected a straightforward plea for cash but this was different. A lively and sinister imagination was at work here.

'I don't live far,' she pleaded.

He realized that it would be rash to go back with her without telling someone at the Yard where he was going. But since Cheadle and Williamson had no idea he was doing this today he could hardly telegraph them, they wouldn't know what he was talking about. Besides, they had no spare men to support him in something he wasn't supposed to be doing in the first place.

What to do?

Having got this far he was reluctant to give up now. He was unlikely to get the chance again. He felt certain that there was something more, much more, at the bottom of all this. Edwin Bennett had gone missing after becoming interested in these advertisements and he had promised his sister Violet that he would try to find out why.

Unlike Edwin, Best reassured himself, he was forewarned and had his warrant card for added protection.

'Very well,' he nodded, 'I'll come.'

Twenty-Nine

Best had been concerned that Mary might take him to Craven Buildings, where he had followed the original Mary. He knew he could not rely on the excitable Harry Rice not to reveal their acquaintanceship.

As it turned out they went almost due north into the Covent Garden Market area although at first that did not appear to be the direction in which they were heading.

Best had purposely not asked their exact destination lest he betray his intimate knowledge of the area by trying to take the shortest and easiest route. That would hardly fit in with his portrayal of himself as a well-to-do and reasonably worldly person who was unacquainted with central London.

They walked down Adelaide Street into the Strand, which as usual at this time of day was caught up in a ghastly traffic tangle due largely to cab and growler drivers bullying their way into the entry gates of Charing Cross Station and out again from its exit gates.

The South-Eastern had managed to build their terminus closer to the heart of London than any of the other railways and had been duly rewarded by a constant flow of passengers to and from Kent – in fierce competition with the London, Chatham and Dover Railway.

The Charing Cross Station Hotel enjoyed similar success, as did Gatti's Music Hall built into the railway arches alongside. Only a few yards further along the Strand they passed Carlo Gatti's confectionery shop. That Swiss-Italian family had certainly made its mark on this part of London. They had now even acquired the Adelphi, one of the Strand's two theatres.

Best's mother had always taken a great interest in the rise of the Gattis. She was fond of pointing out that Carlo Gatti had begun it all with only a coffee and roast-chestnut stall and she held them up as an example of what could be achieved by hard work.

As they walked eastwards along the Strand, Mary kept glancing up at him gratefully. She was certainly more relaxed now, as people are when they have accomplished the most difficult part of their task. But just in case he changed his mind she squeezed his arm now and then and treated him to a winsome smile.

'Left here,' she told him when they reached Bedford Street, adding comfortingly, 'it's not far.'

Walking north now they passed another monument to working-class ingenuity, the old offices of the Civil Service Supply Association. It pleased Best that this huge and splendid building, situated in a street named after the aristocrats who owned the whole area, had grown out of a scheme thought up by a few Post Office clerks who found that tea was cheaper if you bought a chest of it and divided it up amongst yourselves.

Further on they passed Bedford Court and, to the right, Henrietta Street which gave a long view into Covent Garden Piazza and the Flower Market. Then came the tall, elegant gates of Inigo Place, leading through to where gravestones fought for space in St Paul's churchyard.

'Left here,' she said when they reached New Row, a narrow street that during the early hours on market days was packed with jostling carts and vans piled with cabbages and onions, pears and pineapples, lilacs and azaleas.

But it was quiet now.

While Gatti's Gallery Restaurant and Café came alive in the evenings with plotting émigrés and young couples taking tea before attending the nearby theatres it wasn't until after midnight that Covent Garden Market and its surrounding streets began to spring into noisy bustling action when farmers and market gardeners brought in their produce and wholesalers took it away again.

Later came the costermongers and shop-keepers with their smaller carts, then the street flower-sellers to fill up their baskets. They were joined by revellers sobering up in the coffee houses or becoming drunker still in the all-night pubs while prostitutes encouraged them to greater debauchery. Later still came the everyday customers wanting a bunch of roses for a sick relative or to fill their baskets with vegetables which became ever cheaper as the morning wore on.

As New Row narrowed, Mary put out her left hand and said, 'Down here,' and led him into Bedfordbury. Was she trying to confuse him by coming this roundabout way?

The Bedford family were apparently obsessed with putting their names on London streets but in fact this area had been abandoned by them, left out of their seventeenth-century plans for the grand new Covent Garden Piazza and market. Since then it had become a place of such squalor that the whole of the east side of Bedfordbury had just been demolished and replaced by a Peabody Estate of 'homes for the artisan and labouring poor' built by American

254

philanthropist George Peabody.

The west side of Bedfordbury remained untouched. Its numerous dank and narrow alleyways still wended their sordid way through to St Martin's Lane. Mary took him into the first of these, Goodwin's Court, passing under a bridge formed by the upper storey of one of the houses. This 'gate' gave the murky, paved lane a shut-off, secretive air. On the left of Goodwin's Court was a row of quaint but dilapidated bow-fronted shops, now mostly colonized by tailors.

Mary took out a key and let herself in to the third door on the right, climbed the stairs to the second floor, then unlocked the first of two rooms that led off the landing.

A musty smell permeated the tiny room, which had a distinctly uninhabited feel. The furniture was sparse: a narrow little bed, a cheap side table, a flimsy cupboard and a small wooden chair. There was nothing on either the table or cupboard to suggest that a young woman lived here: no hairbrush, trinkets, wash basin and jug, no powder bowl. The only decorative note was provided by a faded papier-mâché screen in the corner of the room.

'Where's the landlord?' Best asked.

'Oh, I'll bring you to him in just a minute,' she said. 'I'll just take off my coat first.'

Since it was almost as cold in there as it

had been outside this seemed pointless.

'Just sit down for a minute.' She pointed to the sole chair, attempting to act the hostess as she unbuttoned her coat, removed and placed it on the bed and said, 'Let me take yours.'

'No need,' he said. 'I won't be here that long, will I?'

She shrugged then in a trice she was behind the screen. Best was taken by surprise. What was she doing? He could scarcely look behind the screen to find out in case she was adjusting her dress in some intimate way.

In fact, he soon discovered, she had been removing it. After a few moments, during which he almost lost sight of her as she bent over unbuttoning things, she emerged clad only in a white corset, chemise and bustle. Her hair was dishevelled and her face quite red. Oh dear.

'There's no need for this,' he insisted. But she seemed not to hear as she untied the tapes of her bustle, let it fall to the ground and looked up at him provocatively.

'Stop it!' he exclaimed. 'Stop this right now.'

But she advanced towards him, put her arms around his neck and stretched up as if to kiss him. Suddenly she withdrew her right arm, reached up and raked her nails down his cheek.

He yelled with pain and anger. 'Why did you do that?'

At that very moment the door opened and a middle-aged, bullish-looking man burst in, took in the scene and shouted, 'My God! What's going on here!'

'That's what I'd like to know!' Best shouted back. He was not sure what to do but his instinct was that equal belligerency was called for. 'And who are you!'

'I'm her husband!' the man shouted

'He tried to rape me!' Mary cried and gave a little sob.

At that the man rushed towards Best, his fists held high.

Best backed against the wall and yelled, 'She's lying!'

He was desperately trying to decide what to do. Should he reveal himself now, even though that would prevent him learning more about their game? The situation was fraught with danger and not just physical. No one at the Yard knew he was here and his excuse 'I was on a case' might seem like just that, an excuse.

'He came to the door, he said he was a gentleman looking for you,' Mary sobbed. 'But when he saw I was alone ... ' Another little sob.

'You bitch!' Best exclaimed, still in character but also speaking personally.

The man's face was now close to his and Best could smell his foul whisky breath. 'Oh, a gentleman, is he? Well, wait till this gets in all the papers. He won't seem such a gentleman then.'

Ah. So it was straightforward blackmail after all. He played his part. 'Oh no! Please! My wife!'

'You should have thought of that before!'

'No! No! Please don't...'

The man stepped back. 'It'll cost you.'

'How much?'

'Two hundred pounds.'

Good grief, they aimed high with their initial payments!

'Well?' said the man contemptuously. 'What's your answer to that?'

Assuming a defeated and humiliated stance Best slipped his right hand into his inside jacket pocket.

The man grinned nastily. 'Singing a different tune now, are we?' He stepped back and relaxed, waiting for Best's wallet to emerge.

Best held his eye with a pathetically pleading expression.

'I haven't got that much on me,' he whined as he brought out a pair of handcuffs, slapped one cuff onto the man's left wrist and fastened the other onto his own right one and announced, 'You are under arrest for blackmail.'

258

The man stared at him, eyes wide, face suddenly grey. Mary's mouth opened and closed emitting small moaning sounds. It was like a tableau vivant, a frozen picture. He turned on her. 'You stupid bitch, bringing him here!'

She cowered against the wardrobe. 'I didn't know. I didn't know. How could I?' she whined.

'Right. Let's go,' said Best decisively and pulled him towards the door, anxious not to allow him too much time to think. When the initial shock wore off he would realize that Best was in a vulnerable position.

Handcuffing yourself to a prisoner could be a dangerous move in a situation like this, particularly when he had an accomplice and there was no help at hand. Best had known colleagues have their noses smashed with their own handcuffs, the dreadful heavy and unwieldy British-made 'flexibles'. Thank goodness his were the latest lightweight American type.

'Come on,' said Best, grabbing the door handle with his left hand.

But the man pushed against the door, a slow cynical smile spreading across his face.

'So,' he said, 'your chiefs won't mind that you attacked a common prostitute...'

Mary looked shocked. 'Sam...' Tears sprang into her eyes. She grabbed her dress and tried to cover herself up.

'Don't use my name, you silly cow!' He turned to Best. 'That will make even better headlines, won't it? Using your authority to kidnap and rape a working girl!'

He is trying to keep me off balance, thought Best, while he decides what to do.

Suddenly, the man's bunched fist came towards him. Best stepped back as far as he could but it still struck the side of his temple, dazing him.

Sam yelled at Mary, who was sitting crouched on the bed weeping, 'Get that knife from the drawer!'

'Don't be stupid,' Best said as he struggled to regain his senses. 'I'm a Scotland Yard detective. Do you imagine I'd come here without support from my colleagues?'

But Mary had the side-table drawer open and was pulling out a long, thin-bladed weapon.

'We've been following your newspaper advertisements for some time. Other detectives followed us, they are waiting out in the street now,' Best went on with a cold and careless confidence he did not feel. 'You'll never escape.'

Sam, knife in hand, hesitated for just a moment too long.

Best's tone grew harsh. 'Now it's only blackmail. But if you murder a policeman you can expect no mercy!'

The man sighed heavily, the bravado gone, threw down the knife and said, 'Oh, all right.'

Before he could reconsider Best hurried him from the room, down the stairs, out into Goodwin's Court and into Bedfordbury. Sam looked around for the other policemen.

'Don't expect to be able to pick them out,' Best warned. 'They are in disguise.' He inclined his head towards two leather-aproned men shouldering barrels of beer to carry across to the cellars of the Lemon Tree public house. 'See that one – ' he nodded at the most muscular drayman – 'he's our shot-putting champion and the other one is our best heavyweight boxer. Half-killed the last man he fought.'

Sensing they were being talked about the first man turned and looked at Best from under the barrel on his shoulder.

'Well done, men,' said Best, giving them a grin and a casual salute with his spare hand as they passed.

They were moving too fast for Sam to notice their bemused expressions and Mary, running to keep up, could see nothing for the tears in her eyes.

Thirty

'Ouch,' said Best. 'That stings!'

'Of course it does, dear,' said Helen, dabbing again at the scratches left by Mary. 'It's meant to.'

He had the uneasy feeling that she was enjoying this, having been furious when she learned of the risks he had taken.

'You'll shorten my life, Ernest Best, making me worry all the time.' She threw the iodine swab into a bin with great venom.

'Nonsense. The excitement keeps you alive.'

She smacked the back of his head. 'You take risks like that again and *I'll* kill you!'

But she had laughed when he told her about the puzzled drayman. 'One of these days, Ernest Best, all that foreign cunning will catch up to you.' She had paused. 'I'd love to have seen their faces!'

Now, she said, 'So, it was only straightforward blackmail after all? No kidnapping or murder of gullible wealthy men?'

He shrugged. 'Seems so. But there may be more to it. Who knows, Edwin Bennett might have fought back and threatened to expose *them*. He didn't have a warrant card to protect him and, if he was as painfully honest as his sister claims, he might have been more interested in the truth coming out than his own reputation.' In Best's opinion unswerving honesty was one of the more overrated virtues.

'And he had no wife to worry about protecting.'

'True. But there was his standing as an upright Christian and pillar of society.'

'I thought he didn't care about "society"?'

'Well, not in the frivolous sense. Anyway, I found none of Edwin Bennett's belongings at Craven Buildings. No body either.'

What they *had* found in Samuel Wickett's rooms at Craven Buildings was the first Mary, who, it seemed, he had not required to meet up with the gentlemen touched by the plight of G.C. but merely to collect the money they sent by post. She, like the other Mary, had been arrested as an accessory to the fraud. He was hoping they might get some more information from her and from them, but so far they were insisting that nothing more than the fraud and blackmail had occurred.

'Poor Violet Bennett. Still left to worry.'

263

'Yes. But at least now I've got a little time to follow that up.'

'No sign of O'Mahoney coming back yet?'

Best shook his head and smiled. 'I enquired about him with the Birmingham detectives and they claim that since Daly's arrest he's gone to ground.'

'In other words, they've lost him like they lost Daly?'

'You're becoming too fluent in police language!' he laughed. 'It's making you cynical.'

But their losing track of Daly might have had a grave outcome. Jenkinson had learned that Daly was about to receive some of those hand grenades intended for the House of Commons.

Fortunately, after the Birmingham police had lost him Daly had been seen by a railway detective at Wolverhampton railway station buying a return ticket to Birkenhead. From there he took the ferry to Liverpool, where he disappeared again.

Spymaster Jenkinson was informed and his deputy, Major Gosselin, sent to lie in wait at Birkenhead. On his return Daly's pockets were found to be bulging with grenades of the most sophisticated design yet. When tested by Colonel Majendie at Woolwich Arsenal the dressmakers' mannequins representing Members of Parliament were slashed to pieces.

'What did Anderson say about all that?'

'He's not there any more. Jenkinson got rid of him.'

'Good heavens. The knives *are* out.' She went over to the studio sink to wash her hands and while she was defenceless Best grabbed her around the waist. She drove him off by splashing him with water.

'The atmosphere between the Home Office and the Yard is terrible and poor old Williamson now has to listen to Jenkinson's words of wisdom instead. But,' he sighed, 'he is the one with the most information now and he says we have to expect more attacks in May.'

'It's strange they can tell you when but not where.' She dried her hands and put her arms around his waist. 'Are they going to give you another Fenian to watch?'

He shook his head. 'Not while I've got these two cases coming up at the Old Bailey. Besides they've decided I'm becoming too well known and I'm even more recognizable now with this.' He pointed to the swelling on his forehead and the livid marks down his cheek made more spectacular by Helen's work with the iodine.

'Well, that's a relief. But you won't take any chances looking for Edwin Bennett, will you?'

'No, I promise,' he said – but he had his fingers crossed.

'There's no telling how long he was down there,' said young Sergeant Mills. 'Most of 'em sink to the bottom straight away an' it's not till they're filled with gas that they come up again and float.'

Best nodded. He refrained from mentioning that he saw more drowned people when he was involved in the *Princess Alice* disaster ten years earlier than a Thames Division officer would in years. People liked to show off their expertise and if you robbed them of the opportunity you could lose useful allies.

'And that takes...'

'Depends on the weather, of course. Quick if it's warm. Slow if it's cold.'

It was the beginning of April but the weather remained quite chilly.

Best inspected what looked like cuts and abrasions on the man's bloated face.

'Those can happen when the body gets pulled along the bottom by the tide,' the sergeant explained, 'or they gets jammed between barges and the like.'

Best preferred not to contemplate the corpse being dragged along the riverbed, the smell and sight were appalling enough. But he nodded his thanks again and asked, 'Where did you find him?'

'We didn't. The dredgers brought him in. They found him off Rotherhithe, an' you know what that means?'

'He could have come from anywhere and there was no money in the pockets when he arrived.'

'That's it.'

Dredgers dragged what saleable flotsam and jetsam they could from the river with trawling nets and were only too happy if that included a body for which they could gain double bounty, the inquest fee and the money from the pockets of the corpse.

Rotherhithe's inquest fee was five times that of next-door Deptford, nobody was quite sure why; but the result was most bodies brought in by dredgers were 'found' at Rotherhithe.

The empty purses usually stayed on the body, as did pocket watches, because both were traceable. This watch certainly was: a large gold triple-calendar hunter with a white-enamelled dial and a cover embellished with a blue-and-white enamel crest of four white plumes clasped by a blue-and-gold-lettered strap.

Best well remembered seeing it in the hand of George R. when he took it out of his fancy grey silk waistcoat pocket in the saloon of the *Calais–Douvres* ferry.

In this instance some money also remained

in the pockets; small-denomination French coins were also identifiable and harder to get rid of than pounds and pence.

Georges Maillet had been found at last.

Thirty-One

Even though Maillet was dead Faucon still refused to lay all the blame on him.

'It was not so,' he insisted. 'I cannot shame his memory with lies.' In vain, Best tried to point out the advantages of him doing so, that is, it might save his life. It would also, of course, mean that the real truth might not be told in court. But Best was of the opinion that in circumstances such as this humanity came before a relentless search for truth. In any case, when had the real truth ever come out in court? Particularly when lawyers began playing their cynical games with the facts?

He and Faucon were sitting side by side on the bench in one of the white-tiled cells at the splendid new Bow Street Magistrates' Court, which adjoined the new police station. They were certainly warmer, cleaner and better ventilated than the dingy and decrepit cells in the old buildings.

'Something I don't understand,' he said, 'is why you stole the watch and his other belongings if it was, as you said, all in self-defence?'

Faucon avoided his eye then lowered his head onto his hands, sat silent for a while then said, 'When we realized what a terrible thing we'd done, we knew that no one would believe that it was in self-defence so, to put you off the scent, we made it look like a robbery.'

'Then you threw him from a moving train,' Best said suddenly angry, 'and spent the money!'

'No! No!' He shook his head. 'The train had stopped. I don't know why, perhaps for another one to pass. Anyway,' he added sadly, 'the man was dead and...'

'No, he wasn't,' snapped Best. 'He came to and crawled along the trackside and through a hole in the fence to escape from you. *Then* he died.'

Faucon moaned. 'Oh, how terrible! How terrible! And he wasn't the wicked man we thought he was. Hang me now! Hang me now!'

'It's all down to mitigation,' Best said to Beauchamp, the French Embassy official trusted to watch the proceedings. 'I can recommend a couple of good mitigation barristers.' The Frenchman had explained that a collection had been made in his home village for Faucon's defence.

Some barristers were brilliant at picking holes in the prosecution case and getting their clients off even though they were obviously guilty. Others, who perhaps were not quite so sharp or as willing to bend the truth, could pluck the heartstrings with excuses for why their clients had been driven to commit the offence. In other words, the mitigating circumstances. Some were no good at either but made a living from those who had never been in trouble before and so had no way of knowing which were the good mouthpieces.

Beauchamp shrugged. 'We already have...'

'I know two who are here today – I'll send them down to talk to him.'

Who knew what kind of barrister the Embassy would produce? A bad one or even one of the mildly incompetent ones could get the man hanged.

Faucon had pleaded guilty but might be persuaded to change his plea. Best thought the evidence against him was too strong for that to be a sensible course. They had been on that train, had changed carriages halfway to a different destination, George R.'s watch and French money had been found on

Maillet and there was Faucon's confession.

If the confession was not disputed, and somehow he doubted it would be, given Faucon's devotion to the truth, he *could* plead not guilty on the grounds of self-defence. But given the state of the body and the fact that there were two of them against one he doubted that any jury would accept that. In fact, it may have been self-defence initially but, Best imagined, in the frenzy of frustration which had overtaken them they had struck out wildly and without mercy. And if he did plead not guilty where then was his mitigation when that plea failed?

'Do these lawyers speak good French?' Beauchamp asked doubtfully.

'Oh, yes,' said Best. 'The barrister will I'm sure and in any case there are perfectly good interpreters.'

This assurance did not appear to convince Beauchamp.

Best was not surprised. The man had over-seen several of the extradition cases at Bow Street where the standard of interpreting was questionable. The principal interpreter was the irascible Mr Albert, a large man who spoke several languages, sometimes mixed them up a little, and had been accused of speaking French with a strong German accent. It didn't help that the acoustics in the splendid new court, with its Portland

271

stone exterior and handsome panelled interiors, were so bad that it was difficult to understand what people said in the first place.

Best pointed out that in this case it did not matter so much since he had pleaded guilty and it would just be a case of taking depositions here to prove a prima-facie case.

'Why doesn't he,' said Best suddenly, changing his mind, 'plead not guilty to murder but guilty to manslaughter – committed due to the misunderstanding? Then mitigating circumstances would emerge at the same time.'

Whose side am I on? he wondered, but consoled himself that George R. would forgive him. As it was, Faucon, seemingly oblivious to his fate, persisted in pleading guilty.

When he had seen Faucon off on his way to the Old Bailey, Best made his way down Wellington Street, passing the Lyceum Theatre, where the return of Henry Irving and Ellen Terry was being heralded by a performance of *Much Ado About Nothing*, crossed the Strand and skirted Somerset House to reach Temple Station on the Thames Embankment. There he caught an underground train for Notting Hill Gate.

Much noise was being made about the fact

that the last link in the Metropolitan and District Railway's Circle Line was to be completed this year but the smoke-ridden atmosphere down there remained choking despite the extra blow holes that had been punched through the worst-offending tunnels, and the lighting in the carriages was as pathetically weak as ever. Nonetheless, the journey was so much quicker and more comfortable than trundling across London on a stop-start omnibus.

Despite the puny light coming from the single lamp in the carriage roof, Best persevered with his newspaper. After combing through the latest intelligence from Egypt and the Sudan, reading the news of the terrible cyclones in America and the speculation on what the next Fenian move would be, he could not resist turning to the personal columns.

Although G.C.'s pleas were no longer featured he had somehow half-expected someone else to pick up that lucrative swindle – perhaps even another participant in the same fraud. He was sure there was more to this whole business than had been revealed by his capture of Sam and the two Marys.

As it was, several other advertisements of dubious intent offered easy ways to make a fortune, win a lover or cure a hopeless malady. But none were very original and he was about to fold the paper and put it away when his strained eyes lit upon a familiar name: Violet Bennett. He sat up and leaned forward to catch as much of the fugitive light as possible and read:

MISSING: Will anyone who knows the whereabouts of Mr Edwin Bennett of Elgin House, Kensington, please contact his sister, Miss Violet Bennett, via her solicitors Messrs. Cundle and Roebottom, 40 Queensway, Notting Hill. If their informations locate the said Mr Bennett a substantial REWARD will be forthcoming. Should Mr Bennett himself see this, please contact your sister to let her know that you are safe.

Poor Miss Bennett. He felt guilty that he had not been back to see her even though it was scarcely his fault. Consequently, instead of going straight home after alighting at Notting Hill Gate he headed for her Bayswater residence.

Initially, Best had the feeling that Violet Bennett was not all that glad to see him, but he reasoned that she might have been otherwise occupied when he called. She was soon smiling her gracious, tranquil smile and assuring him that she was very grateful that he had spared his precious time.

'I'm sorry I haven't been to see you earlier.'

She smiled again. 'Very understandable, with all these outrages. They must keep you very busy.'

'They do. They do.'

'Are you any nearer to catching the culprits?'

He had to admit that they were not. 'But what about your brother? Have you heard anything at all?'

Violet shook her head. She was looking remarkably pretty this evening, he thought, and also rather more fashionable than she had previously.

Her pale-salmon and almond-green dress not only had a draped apron front but a small bustle and was liberally trimmed with crisp white lace and ruby-red velvet ribbon. A confection in fact, and in marked contrast to her previous rather restrained attire. Perhaps her new responsibilities were causing her to blossom? Helen was fond of pointing out that this often occurred when women were given the opportunity to behave like adults instead of idiot children.

'I saw your advertisement in the newspapers.'

She nodded ruefully. 'That's just one of the many ways I've been trying to find Edwin. I have written to anyone I thought had the remotest contact with him; acquaintances, school friends, people he has helped and organizations he was in touch with – even if only occasionally and a long time ago. I have just had a woodcut made of his photograph and printed on bills which are being distributed at railway stations, on cab ranks and all around the area. And, as you suggested, I have employed a private detective.' She sighed. 'It seems so extraordinary that someone could have just vanished like that. It's not as if he is a person without friends, family and contacts.'

Best shrugged. 'A great many people do, I'm afraid. In fact, around eighteen thousand a year. And those are just the reported ones.'

She shook her head. 'How extraordinary.'

'Have you had any response at all so far?'

'No.' She smiled wanly. 'Apart from several communications from the deluded.'

Best grinned. 'We get a lot of those.'

She sighed. 'Oh, and some people have offered to contact him "on the other side".'

Best shook his head. How typical. There was always someone trying to benefit from the misery of others.

'Are many of these eighteen thousand people ever found?' she enquired bleakly.

He nodded. 'About half.'

He failed to add that the bodies of quite a few of the others were pulled out of the Thames or found rotting in some obscure alley and some, though still alive, were destitute and out of their minds.

He was also loath to tell her that the swindlers whom her brother had wanted to help had been arrested. Largely because the arrest had failed to reveal any trace of her brother. Indeed, had somehow shut the door on that possibility. The accused were still denying ever having set eyes on Edwin Bennett. But then if they had done so they were hardly likely to volunteer the information, particularly if they had killed him.

It disturbed him that while the Fenians were distracting them serious crimes might be going undetected. There *was* a possibility of foul play in this case and he should be looking into it further.

She took the news stoically. Doubtless she had become used to these setbacks.

'I won't give up,' she insisted.

In return, he assured her that neither would he, if time and his superiors allowed, and he would see Edwin's name published in police informations.

Helen was not pleased by his late arrival home.

'You said you would be home early

because you were in court all day,' she complained. 'Bessie has had our meal ready for nearly an hour.'

'Sorry, dear. I would have been but on the way home I saw this.'

He took out the newspaper, opened it to the relevant page and showed her Violet's notice. She took it from him with ill grace and began to read. As she did so she raised her eyebrows then put it down and said, 'So...'

'Well, I called on her.'

'I see.'

'I was sorry for her. I felt guilty about not having been back when I promised.'

'You promised *me* that you would be home early. '

Best was indignant. 'I thought you'd be pleased. You were the one who was so worried about us not helping her!'

'I *am* pleased,' she said icily, 'but you might have chosen another time!'

'I couldn't! We're too busy. I never know when I'm going to have the time!'

'If you had to organize household matters as well as to work you'd not be so inconsiderate!'

'And if *you* had to go out to work as a detective you would understand!' Oh dear, this was becoming unpleasant.

'Lucy was very disappointed. I told her you

would have time to play with her.' That was a low blow. She knew it would upset him.

He did not reply but went upstairs to wash and change into more comfortable clothes before coming down to face the icy atmosphere at the dining table. Monosyllabic, coldly polite exchanges followed – 'Please pass the salt', 'May I have the water jug' – until, serving themselves done and eating having commenced, a hostile silence took over.

Eventually, it was broken by Helen. 'So, what did she say?'

He told her. She asked a lot of questions and gradually softened. They never could stay angry with each other for long. Memories of what it was like when they had almost lost each other would come crowding back.

As he suspected, she'd had a bad day at the easel and was behind with her commission. 'I'm sorry,' she said.

'So am I,' he added and blew her a kiss. 'I should have remembered you were expecting me earlier – for once.'

So often she had no idea when he would return.

'It's a pity we don't have a telegraph machine. You could teach Bessie to operate it.'

They both giggled at the idea.

An easier silence fell during which she

began to get that thoughtful look. Eventually she said, 'Has it struck you that there is something a little strange about this business?'

He shook his head. 'Apart from the possibility of foul play by G.C. and company?'

'No, I don't mean that.'

'What, then?' He didn't really want to think about work any more.

'I mean something odd about Miss Bennett's behaviour?'

He shook his head. 'Violet seems to have done everything she could do find her brother.'

'Has she?'

'Yes, she's sent letters, had bills posted all over the place...'

'But she didn't go to the police.'

'*I* went to *her* and she's done all these other things – employed a private detective and...'

'Has she?'

He paused and stared at her, a spoonful of baked semolina pudding halted halfway to his mouth.

'I've no reason to disbelieve her about that.'

'Haven't you? I thought detectives always treated every statement with caution until proven?'

'Yes, but...'

To gain time he waited until he had finished his pudding then said, 'Well, she certainly advertised in the newspapers and...'

'She didn't go to the police,' Helen repeated. The woman could be irritating at times. Had he been a little fulsome about how lovely Violet Bennett looked this evening and described the crimson bows and crisp white lace of her ensemble with a little too much enthusiasm?

'If *you* were *not* a policeman,' she went on relentlessly, 'but a man of some wealth, and you disappeared mysteriously, one of the first things that I would do is go to the police.'

'She sent that letter to G.C. early on and...'

'But that was picked up by you "accidentally",' Helen persisted 'and *she never came back and bothered you again.*' She paused. 'Is that usual?'

He thought about it, waving his hand to refuse a second helping. 'Not with the wealthy,' he admitted finally. It was true. Used to getting their way in all things and imagining the whole world revolved around them they would persist in bothering the police about every minor matter and were, in his opinion, too often indulged in this. 'But she was a woman on her own and didn't know what to do. She wasn't used to being in charge of worldly matters.'

'She had Sidgewick. I understand he is knowledgeable enough?'

'Huh!' exclaimed Best, pushing back his chair. 'He wouldn't want to help her.'

'Are you sure?'

'Oh, of *course*.'

'Is she pretty?'

He stared at her, startled by this sudden diversion.

'*Is she pretty?*' Helen asked again.

He nodded. 'She is now. She's come out of her shell, becoming more vivid. I think she was very sheltered before and timid despite her appearance of calm and self-assurance.'

She was watching him intently.

'I'm sure you would approve of the changes in her,' he added weakly.

'Oh, I do, I do,' she said and smiled teasingly. 'I think she's hoodwinked you.'

Thirty-Two

Next morning Best took another detour, this time to Elgin House to see Sidgewick.

He wasn't exactly sure what he was hoping to discover, perhaps just to learn more about Edwin Bennett and the circumstances of his disappearance and find out whether Sidgewick had any suspicions about Violet.

He did not agree with Helen's doubts about her. She had never met the lady and seen how genuinely worried she was about her brother. If she had, he was sure she would not have persisted with her assertions.

'How long must a person remain missing before their estate goes to the next-of-kin?' she had asked and pointed out that Violet Bennett's enquiries had managed to establish exactly when he had gone missing without instigating a thorough investigation by going to the police.

She kept going back to that. All this 'contact with police' business is making her cynical, he thought. Or was it just plain jealousy? He had to admit that she had shown no signs of that sin previously. Quite the reverse.

'Miss Bennett was relying on me to set it all in motion,' he had insisted. 'She thought I would do all that I could, all that was possible. She is a sensible woman. What would be the point of her harassing me at a time like this when we are so busy? In fact, she did everything she could to assist.'

'Hmm,' Helen had said.

The parlour maid at Elgin House was clearly surprised when he told her his name and his status, and asked to speak to Mr Sidgewick.

'I'll see if he's in, sir,' she said.

'I think you'll find he *is*,' said Best rather firmly.

He was.

'I'll see you through to the drawing room, sir,' she said putting her hand out for his hat then helping him out of his coat. 'Mr Sidgewick will be there very shortly.'

After she had seen him seated and comfortable she left but looked back at him and seemed about to say something. Then she changed her mind and hurried out.

Best was keen to speak to the servants of both households but judged this was not the moment. If she were caught talking out of turn she risked losing her job. He had learned that servants' evidence, should it come to that, did not count for much when defence counsel could portray them as bitter ex-employees. He must find a way to speak to her alone.

He guessed that Sidgewick might be rapidly donning his gentleman's gentleman attire. It would be surprising if, given the time his master had been missing, the man had not relaxed his standards just a little. That would be only human.

As before, however, Elgin House did not appear to have suffered any fall in standards of cleanliness and care. A well-tended, cosy fire still blazed in the hearth, surprisingly welcome on this April day. There were tasteful flower arrangements on side tables glowing from the attentions of some house-maid.

There had been, he noticed, one or two changes in the décor, which was no longer quite so relentlessly masculine. Indeed, there were one or two of what Helen called 'the fripperies' produced by bored ladies of quality: a needlepoint and beadwork cushion on one of the armchairs and a simple water-colour of a pet cat almost covering the space where a larger picture had clearly hung. An oil, if he remembered rightly.

Sidgewick came in, smiling, hand extended in a welcoming fashion, 'Detective Inspector,' he said, 'how nice to see you again. What can I do for you?' For all the world as if he were the man of the house greeting a good friend. Again, not surprising. Hadn't he been placed in that position by the absence of his master?

'It's what I can do for you,' smiled Best. 'I went to see Miss Bennett yesterday and learned from her that her brother is still missing.'

'Yes. Sadly.'

Why did he get the impression that his visit to the Bayswater house was no surprise to Sidgewick?

He really was becoming too suspicious, he decided. Judging the man after having met him only once was not sensible although after so many years' police experience he did imagine himself to be good at spotting a wrong 'un. Not that that had been his conclusion about Sidgewick. He had merely thought that some of his reactions had been a little strange at the time. But now the man looked and acted quite differently. Friendly, alert and ready to listen.

'As I explained to Miss Bennett there is nothing I can do officially as a man is perfectly entitled to leave his past life behind if he wishes. Only if there is good evidence of foul play can we act. However, I saw Miss Bennett's newspaper advertisement so thought I would call on her, and you, to see whether I could assist any more – unofficially, of course.'

'That's very kind of you,' said Sidgewick. 'I'm sure she is very grateful.'

'I understand that Miss Bennett, doubtless with your assistance, has done a great deal to try to trace Edwin by writing to numerous people, having posters put up and hiring a private detective.'

Was it his imagination or had the words private detective come as something of a surprise to Sidgewick?

'She has been wonderful, wonderful,' was his warm response. 'For such a sheltered young lady she has reacted with great courage and determination,' he said and added, 'Her brother would be very proud of her.'

Wait till Helen heard that. An unsolicited recommendation exactly echoing that of Best but coming from a chief manservant, so often arch-enemies of ladies in the family.

'I told her I would circulate Mr Bennett's description in our daily informations.'

He nodded. Again unsurprised.

'That should be very helpful, I'm sure.'

Best wasn't, knowing that hardly any policemen bothered to read them.

It wasn't just Violet's appearance that had changed, Best noted. While Sidgewick's formal black tailcoat did not allow for much show of personal taste, his boots were patent leather and bespoke and, if Best was not very much mistaken, there was something different about his hair. He couldn't quite make out quite what it was, having met the man only once and that briefly, but it somehow looked looser and more expansive. He didn't remember the man's moustache being so curly or his side whiskers being quite so long either.

'What I want to do,' said Best adopting his easiest man-to-man manner, 'is just to go over with you the last time you saw Mr Bennett.'

To his surprise he could have sworn he saw tears start into Sidgewick's eyes, but the man was sitting in the shadow so could not be sure. But was that surprising either? Bonds could grow close even between master and servant, particularly when the employer was one of the better ones.

'How long were you together?'

'Six years.'

'Ah, you must miss him.'

'I do. He was,' Sidgewick pulled himself up, *'is* a kind man and very generous.'

Generous? Why does he want me to know that? 'So I understand from Miss Bennett.' He paused and smiled. 'Better than some employers, I'll be bound?'

'Oh, absolutely.'

'Better than your previous one?'

The manservant inclined his head and gave an apologetic smile as if to indicate that discretion was his stock in trade.

'Who were you with before?' This was something Best wanted very much to know.

'One or two different people.'

'Anyone I know?' Best asked as if seeking salacious gossip about his betters.

'Oh, I shouldn't think so.' He smiled. 'I took a step up when I came to Mr Bennett.'

Ah, he wasn't going to say. I won't pursue it, thought Best. Instead, he grinned in a friendly fashion and said, 'Promotion does give you a satisfying feeling, doesn't it? I wouldn't want to go back to my early days pounding the beat.'

In fact he had rather enjoyed those days; the camaraderie of his colleagues and getting to know the local people on N Division. Sometimes, when a difficult case was troubling him, he almost wished he was back there in Islington where his life had been simpler. But then he would recall the long hours on the beat in all weathers and the frequent spells of boredom.

He went back to the subject of Mr Bennett's last day at Elgin House.

'If we go over it together we might come upon an incident or remark which has been overlooked. Memories have a strange way of

289

coming back a little at a time. Sometimes with a small picture in your mind, sometimes a phrase someone used comes into your head.'

'Strange you should say that,' Sidgewick exclaimed. 'After you had gone the last time I did suddenly recall something.' He held his right hand to his chest to demonstrate the surprise this revelation had caused.

'Oh, yes? What was it?'

'Well...' He paused, for dramatic effect, Best felt. 'That morning he started talking about his will, wanting to change it.'

'That's interesting.' Very interesting. 'Did he say why?'

He shook his head apologetically. 'No.'

'Or in whose favour?'

'No.' He brought his hand to his chest again emphasizing his regret. 'Sorry.'

'Oh, no, don't be. No need. It could be very pertinent about his state of mind.'

'Oh, don't say that!' Again, the hand to the chest, this time pleadingly.

'His solicitor might know. Is he the same one used by Miss Bennett?'

Sidgewick hesitated.

'Cundle and Roebottom of Queensway?' He nodded. 'That's them.'

At the Yard a curious telegraph message awaited Best. It came from the station master of Holborn Viaduct and Ludgate Hill and asked him to go to Ludgate Hill to look at some unclaimed luggage.

What was this all about? More bombs? If so, why ask him to come rather than the City police?

It turned out to be two pieces of luggage that the repository porter had discovered when he eventually got around to searching for suspect bags. Due to the US maker's name on one of the brass locks they had been put to one side as possibly containing dynamite. Later, they had been discounted because one of them, a canvas travelling case with leather handles and straps, was too light to be carrying the deadly substance and the other, a leather Gladstone bag, was not locked and when searched found to hold only private papers, a box of cigars and a travelling clock which had stopped. The canvas case had three initials stamped in gold on its edge: G.R.H.

Once the bags had been brought to the attention of the harassed porter he became aware of them and noticed that several days later they were still just sitting there unclaimed. Having previously been chastised for his dilatory attitude he lost no time in pointing them out to the station master on one of this visits.

He in turn recalled that the suspects in the

murder which had taken place on their railway (a constant topic of conversation among the employees since the discovery of the body and now revitalized since Best had taken Faucon to court) were thought to have diverted on to the city section and alighted at Ludgate Hill. Indeed, this had proved to be the case.

It was of course, Best realized as soon as he set eyes on it, George R. Hardinge's lost luggage. He had wondered what had happened to it having found two small keys on the body that looked like luggage keys. But he had quite overlooked the fact that the Frenchmen too might think of leaving it at the station for collection later. They may have picked it up to give themselves more of the appearance of respectable travellers and then either decided to get rid of it or left it for collection. Removing it from the murder scene had certainly delayed the identification of the person who had been in the bloody compartment. Perhaps that was their intention as well?

Why didn't I ask Faucon about it, he thought, instead of worrying about the man's defence? I'm not doing my job properly.

'Don't be so hard on yourself,' Helen said. 'You have been distracted by other matters.'

'Yes,' he said morosely. 'Some I shouldn't have been doing.'

He had in mind all this running around after the elusive Edwin Bennett, who had probably just decided to leave his past life behind as so many others did. He had never received an official docket assigning the case to him. He had just been indulging his curiosity.

Helen would have none of it. She was in a good mood since he had managed to get home in time to read Lucy one of her favourite stories. He also had brought her a spinning top which, while she was far too young to play with it yet, made her squeal with delight when he whipped it into a multicoloured whirlwind. She had become over-excited and tried to grab at the whizzing object but it had all ended in gurgles and giggles before she went happily to bed in her daddy's arms.

As soon as they had settled down for a chat before dinner Helen asked about his visit to Elgin House. She was not the least bit surprised that Sidgewick had given Violet Bennett such a warm recommendation.

'Who knows what they are up to,' she said, picking up some sewing. 'Sharing the inheritance?' She paused. 'Did you ask whether Edwin had any lady friends?'

Best nodded. 'Yes. He insisted that there

were none. Apparently, Edwin was very shy with women. There had been a quiet romance a couple of years ago with a childhood friend.'

'What happened?'

'It died out. Well, not exactly died out,' Best corrected himself. 'He hadn't acted quickly enough. The woman wasn't sure of his intentions so she went off and married another rich young man. After that he put all his energies into good works.'

'Hmm,' said Helen as she selected the right thread from her needlework box. While she scorned the producers of antimacassars and beaded cushions she quite enjoyed a little practical sewing. 'Did you speak to any of the servants?'

'No. But the parlour maid almost told me something when I went in and as she gave me my coat on the way out she kept looking as if she wanted to say something. Unfortunately, just then Sidgewick came to see me out so she couldn't.'

'Are you going to go back to try to speak to her outside?'

He shrugged. 'I haven't the time. I've wasted too much on this already. Cheadle was irritated because I was late today.'

'Would you like me to...'

'No!' he shouted. 'Don't you dare!'

They'd had one experience of Helen 'helping' which had almost been the death of her. Him too. He wondered again whether it was wise to tell her so much.

'Anyway, I managed to drop one of my cards into her apron pocket without him seeing.'

'Good for you!'

One other thing had happened which, despite his misgivings he couldn't resist telling her.

'As I was walking away down Addison Road I looked back and I saw a carriage stop outside Elgin House.'

He had her attention. That's why he did it, she was such a good audience. So curious.

'And...'

'Don't keep me in suspense, you irritating man...'

'Who should get out but Miss Violet Bennett.'

Her eyes opened wide. 'Good heavens!' she exclaimed. 'They must be lovers!'

Thirty-Three

During the next few weeks Best had little time to contemplate the disappearance of Edwin Bennett, his time being fully taken up with the trials and more Fenian-watching.

He'd dismissed straight away Helen's ridiculous notion that Violet Bennett and Sidgewick could be conducting a romance. She would never take to a man like that! Sidgewick might be clever and have a veneer of cultivation but there was something about him that remained uncouth and calculating. Besides, he was a servant and Miss Bennett, although very gracious, was, he was sure, a very conservative young lady in that respect.

Helen had laughed and said the contrast would be the attraction and didn't he realize that some people saw their marriage like that?

There had probably been a quite innocent reason for Violet Bennett's visit to Elgin House that morning. After all, they were both searching for her brother so even if she *had* gone to report on his visit to her it would have been a natural thing to do. And there was the fact that since he acted as Edwin's steward she would doubtless consult him about financial affairs.

It was true that the few feminine changes he had noted in the house might well be due to her influence. But why not? If Edwin did not return she would be taking over as mistress.

All the more reason for Sidgewick to consolidate his position by gaining her personal approval, Helen had said. He smiled and admitted to himself that Helen's assumptions may have had more to do with his own dramatic presentation of the situation than the reality of it.

The night before he went to court for Faucon's trial, Best read through the report on the state of the French wine industry that George R. Hardinge had been compiling for the US government. It was a follow-on to a report they had commissioned, among several others, when they had been rebuilding their country after the devastation caused by the Civil War. While some had gone abroad to observe advances in railway engineering and various industrial processes this deputation had been sent to study wine. But things had changed since then.

George R.'s report (which he had probably

been working on in the train that day, judging by the fact that the Gladstone bag which held it was unlocked) was wide-ranging and thorough. It pointed out that even before the advent of phylloxera not all had been well due to complications of the European free-trade policies and a run of bad weather. There was also the agricultural depression, brought on in part by importation of cheap grain from the United States, which in turn had led to a decline in wine-drinking in important markets like Great Britain.

He had gone on to describe the present situation, which, he said, was dire. In his opinion it could only be reversed by whole-sale grafting onto US rootstock and, considering that the plague had come from the United States (though no blame was attached to them) the US government should do all they could to support the recovery. He went on to describe how they might do this.

Best realized that the report would neither be of comfort to Faucon nor assistance to himself so he decided to show it to the defence counsel and his junior only if they asked for it. In the event they did not.

The Frenchman had after all been persuaded by him to plead guilty to manslaughter 'for the sake of his family'. Thus he escaped the death penalty and was given a life sentence instead. Best had hopes that after the story was revealed in his barrister's dramatic mitigation plea he would be allowed, as requested, to serve the latter part of his sentence in France. After all, leaders of the planned uprising in Ireland in 1865 had been amnestied after a few years on the provision that they left the country and *they* had been charged with treason-felony.

Scotland Yard had been warned to expect more explosions during the month of May but it was already the thirtieth and there had been no sign. Perhaps the Fenians had changed their plans? Or, the optimists at Scotland Yard and the Home Office hoped, abandoned them altogether after the grenades were found at Birkenhead and the railway-station bombings proved only partially successful.

That evening, Best left the Yard early after having worked many late nights on Fenian enquiries. Just before eight o'clock music-loving Detective Chief Inspector Littlechild also left – for the opera. He was in the habit of working late these days but a friend had given him the tickets. Detective Sergeant George Robson and Kerry-born Detective Inspector John Sweeney worked on. Soon, only Sweeney was left, but at nine o'clock he too called it a day and left the office of the

Special Irish Branch.

Twenty minutes later, a bomb exploded in the urinal which stood outside the office. It demolished the wall, destroying the desk at which Sweeney had been working and many papers relating to Fenian activities. It also wrecked the glittering front of the Rising Sun public house opposite, sending shards and splinters of plain and decorative glass in every direction.

The constable charged with keeping a lookout for suspicious persons carrying suspicious packages was cut about the face and head by flying debris and promptly became deaf. Two drivers awaiting fares outside the Rising Sun also received injuries, one suffering a broken arm. Their hansom cabs were wrecked, but their horses, though shocked, were relatively unscathed.

It was not the only explosion in Central London that night. Two minutes earlier two more had disturbed the peace of the élite residents and clubmen of St James's Square. The first had been placed in the basement area in front of the kitchens of the Junior Carlton Club, injuring twelve employees. The second erupted on a windowsill at the house of a Member of Parliament. In this case, despite the flying glass and masonry, the only injury suffered by the party assembled within was a minor cut to a lady's hand.

The servants, however, were not so fortunate. Two of them, who had been standing on the doorstep, were injured, one, it was later reported, 'somewhat seriously'.

The threat was not yet over. While confusion reigned at Scotland Yard a boy found a black bag lying close to one of the lions at the base of Nelson's column in Trafalgar Square. To topple this English hero would have been a Fenian triumph. Inside the bag was found eight-and-a-quarter pounds of lignine dynamite known as Atlas Powder 'A'.

The following evening Eliza Bertram, parlour maid at Elgin House in Kensington, arrived at Scotland Yard, where she asked to speak to Inspector Best.

Thirty-Four

It was clear that Eliza wished she had not come to Scotland Yard. In fact, by the time Best reached her she was standing up, had drawn the strings of her handbag tight, slipped them back over her wrist and was ready to make her excuses and leave.

She looked vulnerable and uncertain without her armoury of frilled cap and apron and specific tasks to perform. Her speech too had become stilted as she tried to tell him what a mistake it had been and that she was sorry to have troubled him.

Best was familiar with the symptoms and immediately began to converse with her as though she was an old friend and it was the most natural thing in the world for her to call in to a half-wrecked Scotland Yard as she was passing.

They were sitting in a room in the main building which looked out towards the Special Irish Branch office and which itself had lost no fewer than fifty-two windows.

'Sorry about the mess,' Best said, pointing to the pile of glass on the floor beneath the boarded-up window. 'They haven't had time to clear up this room yet.'

'That's all right,' she said. 'Terrible, wasn't it. Was anybody hurt?'

'Only slightly,' he said.

'That's why I came,' she said suddenly. 'Not to *see* it,' she added hurriedly. 'Just hearing about it reminded me and I said to myself, Lizzy, I said, "You've got to go. You're being a coward not going." ' She paused. 'I've kept meaning to,' she insisted, 'but I'd get scared, and I kept thinking maybe I'm wrong. That I was imagining things and Mr Bennett would be back tomorrow...'

'Well, you're here now,' Best said and patted her arm. 'If there's nothing to it, it won't matter, will it?' He paused. 'Tell me why you've come.'

'Well,' she said, 'he was such a nice man.'

Best had been eager to hear a disinterested opinion of Edwin Bennett but had the feeling that what was about to follow was much more important. Nonetheless, he realized he must take Eliza at her own pace.

'In what way?'

'Well, he always said, "Good morning, Eliza" and "Good evening, Eliza" and asked you how you were and said nice things about what you'd done.'

This man was a man who was shy of women? Perhaps, like some, he felt more at ease with servants than he did with ladies of a higher station in life? Perhaps he didn't just give them pretty compliments but formed alliances or even took advantage of them? It was a common enough situation.

But Best asked, 'Tell me about Mr Bennett's friends. Did he have a special lady friend?'

'Oh no!' she exclaimed. 'He wasn't like *that*!' She put her hand to her mouth and blushed to the roots of her hair. 'I mean...' She struggled to find the words but failed.

Best changed direction. 'Where do the servants live? Up in the attic?'

'Oh no, we don't!'

'Where, then?'

'We don't live in.'

That was unusual. Servants living out in a house like that.

'None of you? Not even the butler and the housekeeper?'

She shook her head. 'Only Mr Sidgewick.'

'Oh, I see.'

He was beginning to.

When it finally spilled out, the words tumbled over each other. 'We didn't think nothing of it, you see, but then once when I stayed late to set up the table for the morning I went into the breakfast room...' She was becoming agitated, reliving the experience. 'You see, I thought there was no one there any more and...' she said as though excusing herself to him. 'And then...' Her hands flew to her face again as she tried to frame the words to describe what she had seen.

'What was it?' asked Best crisply. There came a moment when it was necessary to prise the words out of a witness.

Her eyes and mouth were open wide. Finally she exclaimed, 'They were kissing!' She wrung her hands. 'Mr Sidgewick and Mr Bennett were kissing! And that wasn't all! I didn't know where to look. But they were so ... so ... They didn't see me.' She lowered her voice to a whisper. 'So I sneaked out, quiet as I could, and ran all the way home.'

Best didn't say anything. This put a whole new complexion on things. If only she had come earlier.

'My Henry said they must be Mary Anns and not to say anything to anyone 'cos they would go to prison and I would lose my job.'

Having got the general picture, Best did not press her any further on the subject. 'Tell me about the day Mr Bennett disappeared.'

'We never saw him at all that day. When we got in that morning, he just wasn't there.' She frowned. 'And we always got in before Mr Bennett got up. But he just wasn't there. At first Mr Sidgewick didn't say anything then he began to ask us if we'd seen him, but we hadn't.'

Best pondered this for a moment then asked, 'What about the night before? Was he there when you left?'

She nodded. 'Oh, yes. But they weren't speaking to each other and the cook said she'd heard them having a terrible row that afternoon out in the garden. She said she was amazed that Mr Sidgewick dared to shout at Mr Bennett like that.'

'Did she hear what was said?'

She shook her head. 'Mrs Bailey's a bit deaf. But she knew he was shouting all right.'

'Anything else?'

She shook her head. 'Henry said I shouldn't say nothing about any of it. Keep out of it, he said. But he was such a nice man and I was worried he might have done something to himself. He must have been very upset to leave like that without telling no one. You would think it would be Mr Sidgewick who would have gone if anyone did, wouldn't you?'

Best nodded. 'You would. You did well to come in,' he said, 'and don't worry, I won't say anything to Mr Sidgewick.' He would, however, be having a serious talk with him regarding 'rumours he had heard in the neighbourhood'.

As she reached the door she stopped suddenly and said, 'Oh yes, I forgot. There *was* one other thing. That day he wasn't there the cellar door was locked. Mr Sidgewick said that Mr Bennett must have taken the key with him. He went down there sometimes to choose the wine. The footman said he could get it open without the key but Mr Sidgewick said not to bother just now. He didn't want the lock ruined and to wait till Mr Bennett came back. He said he was probably with some friends in the country. He'd spoken about going there and that there was plenty of wine upstairs for now.'

'When was the door opened again?'

'About a week after Mr Bennett left.' She paused. 'We thought it peculiar that Mr Sidgewick didn't have another key.'

So do I, thought Best.

'He said he'd lost it. But that weren't like him, really.'

Best did not prove to be a very popular person in the wrecked Scotland Yard offices when he announced that he probably had another murder enquiry on his hands and needed help with it.

'Where is it and what is it?' asked Cheadle ungraciously, as if Best were deliberately finding these cases to throw the Yard into even deeper confusion. They were much occupied with trying to find ways to explain how they had allowed a bomb to be planted right under their noses at the very offices where the war upon the Fenians was supposedly being brought under control. The atmosphere with the Home Office was awful although Jenkinson was gleeful about their predicament.

One thing was certain, they needed every available man to track Fenians, guard important personages and prevent bombs being placed under London's bridges or thrown into the Houses of Parliament.

When Best told him it was in Kensington,

by Holland Park, he grunted sourly, 'The divisionals can 'andle it,' ignoring the fact that their numbers were also depleted – for the same reasons.

Best cleared his throat. 'If we had something of a hand in it, it might take people's minds off the bombs and give us some good publicity.'

Cheadle grunted again. He wasn't usually bothered about such matters but even he had been embarrassed about being caught napping. 'Oh, all right,' he said. 'But only for a couple of days until you can hand over. An' you better eat 'umble pie. They'll not be pleased that you've been messing about in their manor without telling them.'

Best nodded and said testily, 'I had every intention of being diplomatic.' Messing about!

Cheadle looked at him over his half spectacles then said, 'You can take Smith. But only for a couple of days.'

'Thank you, sir.'

That was obviously the nearest he was going to get to a pat on the back.

When Sidgewick saw all the policemen, some of them armed with pickaxes and shovels, he looked astounded. Then he saw Best, glared at him and exclaimed, 'What's this all about, officer!'

Best showed him the warrant and told him what they were about to do. He stood there without moving, just staring at them. Then he sighed, opened the door wide to let them in and even led them to the cellar.

'I loved him,' he told Best, who stayed with him in the drawing room while the local police got to work. 'But *he* didn't love *me*, not really. He just wanted someone and I was there.'

Apparently, that was what the argument in the garden had been about. In a way.

'He said it was over. I asked if there was someone else but he denied it. Said he'd never done anything like this before and now he was ashamed. It was sinful and he couldn't carry on. Said he'd give me a good reference. As if that was all there was to it!' He stopped as tears brimmed into his eyes.

Oh dear, thought Best, another tearful male. He could cope with weeping females but...

'That's when I picked up the poker and began to hit him with it,' Sidgewick exclaimed vehemently. He looked down at the offending hands. 'Couldn't stop.'

The divisional detective inspector put his head around the door and nodded.

'Why is it always the cellar?' Helen asked.

'It isn't,' Best said. 'But it's hard to hide a

body with so many servants coming in the morning. He could hardly start digging up the garden in the dead of night.'

'You only have his word on what the argument was about.'

'Of course. But I doubt if we will get any other account now unless one of the other servants "remembers" having heard what was said.'

'So, Edwin was not a victim of G.C. and Samuel Wickett after all?'

He shook his head, 'No, and the joke is...' He paused and took off his hat and gloves.

'What?' She waved her paint brushes about in frustration. 'The joke is what?'

'The joke is,' he said drawing it out while she made faces at him, 'that he may not have even *seen* the advertisement. Sidgewick did and thought that telling Violet that her brother might have gone to see G.C. seemed like a good way to divert her attention. But, of course, what it did was cause her to blossom and start taking on responsibilities.'

'Ah, yes. Violet Bennett.'

'Well?' asked Best.

'Well, what?'

'Are you going to admit that you were wrong about her?'

'In what way?' She gazed up at him innocently.

'Saying that she hoodwinked me. That she

310

was up to something. That they were lovers...' He paused. '*That* way.'

She shrugged. 'Well, I was only helping you out. *You* didn't seem to have any better ideas – even though *you're* supposed to be the detective.' She paused then added brazenly, 'After all, you can't expect me to solve all your cases for you!'

She held her paint-clogged brushes up in front of her for protection as he advanced relentlessly towards her. Then, sensing defeat, she flung them into the sink and ran.

Thank goodness *we* don't have a houseful of servants, Best thought, when he caught her and took his revenge.

Author's Note

The 'outrages' described in this book were all real, as were the police and Home Office personnel Vincent, Williamson, Moser, Littlechild, Anderson and Jenkinson and all the Fenians apart from O'Brien, Flinn and O'Mahoney.

On 10 December 1884, three members of the Clan na Gael blew themselves up while planting a bomb under London Bridge. On 2 January 1885, a bomb exploded in a tunnel of the Metropolitan Railway between King's Cross and Gower Street, causing minor casualties. Three weeks later, on 24 January, a bomb exploded in the armoury of the Tower of London, injuring four people, and almost simultaneously a parcel burst into flames in the medieval crypt of the House of Commons. This exploded whilst being carried upstairs by a policeman, who was injured. But it was only a diversionary tactic; the real bomb erupted in the Commons chamber shortly afterwards. It caused much damage but, since Parliament was not sitting, no one was hurt.

Back at the Tower of London the gates were immediately closed and police questioned everyone present until they came across a man with an American accent. He turned out to be a Clan na Gael member, James Gilbert Cunningham. He was found guilty of planting that bomb and the one on the Metropolitan Railway, while Harry Burton, a colleague traced through him, was convicted of planting some of the left-luggage bombings of the previous year.

The Home Office Spymaster General, Edward Jenkinson, continued his war against Scotland Yard. He sent his spies racketing around London, Paris, New York and Sweden, causing problems for the police and acting as agents provocateur in various dynamite plots. Eventually, he became such an embarrassment that he was sacked.

In 1886, the bombing stopped abruptly while the Home Rule Bill was being considered and, possibly, also due to the continued opposition from the Irish Republican Brotherhood and the capture of so many of the bombers.

Wrangles between Fenians continued, and in 1888, accusations of misappropriation of funds by one section of Clan leaders, particularly their leader Alexander Sullivan, came to a head. A Clan 'trial' was held which exonerated them, but one ex-member, Dr Patrick Cronin, refused to hold his tongue. He was murdered (horrifically, with ice picks) the following year. Three Clan members were found guilty of the killing but the case against Sullivan and one other was dropped due to lack of evidence.

Also in 1889, a Special Commission was set up in London to examine allegations that Irish MP Charles Stewart Parnell had been aware of Fenian plots including the one to assassinate the Queen during her Golden Jubilee celebrations (the actual bombers had been arrested and convicted before they could act).

A shock witness before the Commission was an Englishman, Thomas Billis Beach alias Henri Le Caron who, after serving in the US Civil War, had joined the Fenian Brotherhood. For many years he was at the heart of their organization while regularly sending information regarding their plans back to Anderson in London.

It is chilling to read his account of the second Fenian invasion of Canada, for which he was made a brigadier general in the Fenian army and which he had betrayed. In his book, *Twenty-Five Years in the Secret Service*, he reports himself amused by the Fenians' certainty that they would take the Canadians by surprise and rapturously describes the beautiful Canadian landscape where he saw them ambushed then retreating 'leaving their dead to be subsequently buried by the Canadians'.

Of course, the whole Fenian story is much more complex than can be conveyed here. Many books have been written on the subject. Two I found particularly useful are *The Dynamite War: Irish American Bombers in Victorian Britain* by K. R. M. Short and the more recent *Fenian Fire* by Christy Campbell.

As for the phylloxera saga, grafting eventually overtook sulphurism, and by 1893 the French wine industry had recovered sufficiently for the harvest to exceed pre-phylloxera levels. The aphid is still with us worldwide, however, and small outbreaks continue, as does research on the subject. Again, this is a complex story which is thoroughly told by Christy Campbell in *Phylloxera: How Wine was Saved for the World*.

Today, the French wine industry is struggling in some areas due both to their own countrymen cutting down on their wine consumption for health reasons and their wines having been ousted from first place in the British wine market by those from Australia and New Zealand.

The war between the London, Chatham and Dover and the South-Eastern railways

315

finally ended when they joined forces in 1899 to form the South-Eastern and Chatham Railway.

Finally, much of the information regarding Scotland Yard detectives stems from my research for two of my non-fiction books: *Dreadful Deeds and Awful Murders: Scotland Yard's First Detectives 1829–1878* and *Scotland Yard Casebook: The Making of the CID 1865–1935*. Also helpful were *The Reminiscences of Chief-Inspector Littlechild*, 1894, and *Stories from Scotland Yard* by Inspector Moser, 1890. In fact, I confess that G.C.'s letter to the newspapers was lifted almost verbatim from the former.